COOK THE BOOKS

COOK THE BOOKS

Jessica Conant-Park

& Susan Conant

BERKLEY PRIME CRIME, NEW YORK

THE BERKLEY PUBLISHING GROUP
Published by the Penguin Group
Penguin Group (USA) Inc.
375 Hudson Street, New York, New York 10014, USA
Penguin Group (Canada), 90 Eglinton Avenue East, Suite 700, Toronto, Ontario M4P 2Y3, Canada
(a division of Pearson Penguin Canada Inc.)
Penguin Books Ltd., 80 Strand, London WC2R 0RL, England
Penguin Group Ireland, 25 St. Stephen's Green, Dublin 2, Ireland (a division of Penguin Books Ltd.)
Penguin Group (Australia), 250 Camberwell Road, Camberwell, Victoria 3124, Australia
(a division of Pearson Australia Group Pty. Ltd.)
Penguin Books India Pvt. Ltd., 11 Community Centre, Panchsheel Park, New Delhi—110 017, India
Penguin Group (NZ), 67 Apollo Drive, Rosedale, North Shore 0632, New Zealand
(a division of Pearson New Zealand Ltd.)
Penguin Books (South Africa) (Pty.) Ltd., 24 Sturdee Avenue, Rosebank, Johannesburg 2196,
South Africa

Penguin Books Ltd., Registered Offices: 80 Strand, London WC2R 0RL, England

This book is an original publication of The Berkley Publishing Group.

This is a work of fiction. Names, characters, places, and incidents either are the product of the author's imagination or are used fictitiously, and any resemblance to actual persons, living or dead, business establishments, events, or locales is entirely coincidental. The publisher does not have any control over and does not assume any responsibility for author or third-party websites or their content.

PUBLISHER'S NOTE: The recipes contained in this book are to be followed exactly as written. The publisher is not responsible for your specific health or allergy needs that may require medical supervision. The publisher is not responsible for any adverse reactions to the recipes contained in this book.

Copyright © 2010 by Jessica Conant-Park and Susan Conant.
Interior text design by Kristin del Rosario.

FIRST EDITION: March 2010

Library of Congress Cataloging-in-Publication Data

Conant-Park, Jessica.
    Cook the books / Jessica Conant-Park & Susan Conant. — 1st ed.
        p. cm.
    ISBN 978-0-425-23246-0
    1. Carter, Chloe (Fictitious character)—Fiction. 2. Cooks—Fiction. 3. Boston (Mass.)—Fiction.
I. Conant, Susan, 1946– II. Title.
    PS3603.O525C66 2010
    813'.6—dc22   2009041626

PRINTED IN THE UNITED STATES OF AMERICA

10 9 8 7 6 5 4 3 2 1

In loving memory of Lynne Frey

Acknowledgments

As always, many thanks to those who contributed incredible recipes: Authors J. B. Stanley and Mia King, and chefs Justin Hamilton, Bill Park, and Jonathan Sawyer.

A definite nod to our favorite Desperate Chef's Wife, Hilary Battes, and to the Chef's Widow, Amelia Zatik Sawyer, who both run phenomenal Web sites that chronicle life with chefs. Stop by www.desperatechefswives.com and www.chefswidow.com for a good laugh (and maybe a tear or two).

A huge hug to Michele Scott, who lets Jessica call her three times a day for support and advice about nearly everything.

Thanks again to our fabulous agent, Deborah Schneider, and to Natalee Rosenstein and Michelle Vega from Berkley for all of their hard work.

COOK THE BOOKS

ONE

I have a love-hate relationship with Craigslist. On the one hand, I adore poking through the online classifieds for items I don't even want—Swedish bobbin winders, chicken coops, vintage Christmas ornaments—and for enviable extravagances that I can't afford—such as the services of someone to come to my house to change the cat litter. On the other hand, I hate getting sucked into the vortex of randomly searching for weird items and unaffordable services instead of looking for what I actually need. For example, at the moment, I absolutely had to find a part-time job. I leaned back into my couch and adjusted the laptop so that it balanced comfortably on my knees.

I was broke because of the cutest baby in the world,

Patrick, the three-month-old son of my best friend, Adrianna. One day last August, Adrianna and her husband, Owen, had almost simultaneously gotten married and become parents, and since then I'd spent a small fortune spoiling them and Patrick. Ade was staying at home with the baby while Owen, a seafood salesman, struggled to support them. Driving around Boston in a refrigerated truck, Owen delivered fish and shellfish to restaurants and tried to get new accounts. He seemed to spend as much on gas as he made on commissions. Luckier than Adrianna and Owen, I had a monthly stipend that was deposited into my account, courtesy of my late uncle Alan, but the money hadn't begun to cover the cost of my recent expenditures. As pleased as the credit card company must have been about the interest I was paying, its representatives were equally displeased with my making sporadic and late payments.

The principal blame for the hideous state of my finances lay with high-end baby boutiques and the baby sections of beyond-my-means department stores. How could I resist the designer blankies, the infant activity centers, the fancy play saucers, the darling Ralph Lauren outfits, and the endless assortment of rattles? Plus, Patrick obviously needed the expensive machine that reproduced the natural sounds of the jungle, the ocean, and evening in the forest, right? Ade and Owen lived in a cramped one-bedroom apartment around the corner from mine. Patrick's room had once been—and in reality still was—a closet; granted, it had a window and a radiator, but a closet it remained. So, the least I could do for my favorite friends was to lavish upon them everything they needed for their cherished and irresistible son, who was also my godson.

My spending had a second explanation, one much less altruistic than the desire to indulge my friends. As I hated to admit even to myself, my transformation into an especially profligate spendthrift just had to represent some sort of effort to fill the void that my boyfriend Josh had left when he'd moved to Hawaii. Yes, incredible though it still seemed, my perfect, gorgeous, charming, adorable chef boyfriend, Josh Driscoll, had up and left Boston to work as a private chef for a family in Hawaii. As of mid-September, we would have been together for a year. But instead of celebrating our anniversary with Josh, I'd spent most of September either shopping like a maniac or curled up in a ball on the couch, crying my eyes out. On Adrianna's wedding day, the same day that she'd given birth to Patrick, Josh had asked me to go to Hawaii with him. Dream come true, right? Well, maybe for someone else, but I'd been heartbroken and furious at the invitation. There was no way that I wanted to leave Adrianna, Owen, and their new baby. Furthermore, I was just beginning the second year of my master's degree program in social work. I hadn't exactly been a highly motivated student during my first year, but I was belatedly starting to fit in at social work school and to realize that my choice of the field had been far less random and capricious than I'd originally thought. In fact, I was enjoying my work too much to drop everything and jet off to Hawaii. Besides, it seemed to me that Josh's decision to leave was an impulsive reaction to the tumultuous year he'd had, a year of bouncing from one disastrous restaurant experience to another. He'd been chronically overworked and exhausted, stressed beyond imagination, and the opportunity to work in Hawaii must have seemed like an easy way out. I just wished that, given the choice between Hawaii and me, he'd chosen me.

Josh had continued to e-mail me and occasionally to call, but I ignored his attempts to explain himself, deleted his messages, and eventually blocked his address altogether. It was now November, and I was no longer willing to hang around my condo, pining for a lost love. I had a life to live, and I was not going to be one of those women whose entire life hinges on a relationship with some guy. Even if that guy was the best thing that had ever happened to me! No, I, Chloe Carter, was an independent woman, a loyal friend, and a driven graduate student!

I again focused on Craigslist and clicked back to the main job categories in search of something that might pique my interest. "Accounting+finance" sounded relevant to my situation, but the state of my bank account hardly qualified me to manage someone else's finances. "Arch / engineering" sounded high paying, but my experience in the field was limited and unpromising. When I'd helped Owen to assemble Patrick's crib, I'd failed to insert two long pieces of wood that had turned out to be major support bars. I really wasn't equipped to apply for any sort of job involving architecture or engineering. "Internet engineers" sounded important and interesting, but my principal Internet skill consisted of expertise in Googling old classmates to see who had done anything Nobel Prize—worthy or scintillatingly illegal, so that I could feel either pitifully unsuccessful or smugly superior by comparison. I also spent time on the Web researching term papers and browsing for recipes and food trivia, but those activities hardly made me an Internet engineer.

4

Aha! "Food / bev / hosp" sounded more up my alley! I hesitated for a second because of Josh, who'd been one reason for my spending the past year totally consumed by all things food and chef related. I reminded myself, however, that I'd been a foodie *before* Josh and that I could continue to love all things gastronomic *after* Josh. Ugh. *After Josh.* I hated the sound of the words. I was over him. I had to be. I had no choice. And if searching through food-industry jobs was my way of clinging to the past? Well, avoiding the industry would mean that I was running away from it because I was still hurting, as I undeniably was. Every piece of cooking equipment in my kitchen reminded me of Josh. I was sick of tearing up at the sight of a measly spatula and cursing every time I turned on the oven. I damned well was going to get over crying at the sight of wooden spoons and paring knives! Maybe working in the food industry was exactly what I needed. Yes, I'd flood myself with food images until I was no longer reminded of Josh! I scrolled through the listings, but all of the jobs turned out to be for servers, cooks, bar managers, and mixologists. I don't know what I'd been hoping for. A job as a voracious eater? As a taste tester?

I returned to the main menu. "Skilled trade"? How humiliating to realize that I had no skills! Even so, I skimmed the page and found "writing / editing." I'd certainly written and edited plenty of my own papers over the past year. Although I couldn't be considered a professional writer, I could probably pass myself off as preprofessional or possibly as just on the verge of becoming professional or as all but professional, so close to being outright professional that no one could tell the difference. Anyhow, it would certainly be easier to sell a potential employer on my writing skills than it would be to pretend that I possessed a "skilled trade" or that I was really quite qualified to serve as a mixologist or an architect or an Internet engineer. Skimming the writing and editing jobs, I discovered that I was impossibly unqualified for many. The odds of my suddenly becoming a Portuguese-English bilingual person who could prepare scholarly bibliographies were slim to none. And I was not about to attempt to edit a math textbook.

One job, however, leapt off the screen: assistant to a cookbook writer! The listing said the applicant would need solid writing skills in addition to an enthusiasm for food and recipes. The job was tailor-made for me! I immediately e-mailed my résumé and a quick letter of introduction that explained my unabashed love for everything that had anything to do with food. Then I crossed my fingers. This was the one and only job I'd applied for, mainly because it was the only one that interested me. Incidentally, it also happened to be the only job on Craigslist that I could possibly perform. Who knew what it would pay, though? Furthermore, if the job was so appealing to me, it might be equally so to others, meaning that I'd face serious competition.

I shut down the computer and headed down the short hall that led to my kitchen. As usual, the prospect of walking in felt like going into battle. The appliances, the food, and the utensils all seemed to be taunting me, reminding me of my chef. Truthfully, my whole condo reminded me of Josh, especially because we'd spent much more time at my place than at his. I loved my condo, and I wanted to feel the way I used to feel about it, but even my wall colors made me think of Josh. I'd gone through a serious phase of impulsively painting and repainting each room a different earthy color, and Josh had fueled my interest by giving me painting supplies as my Christmas gift last year. Maybe I'd have to repaint yet again. We'd spent hours snuggling on the couch in the tiny living room, and I'd watched him cook countless meals in my kitchen. And the bedroom? Well, there was the bedroom, too. One of my cats, Inga, brushed against my leg as I stood in the entryway to the kitchen. Josh had rescued Inga from a horrible owner who had threatened to toss her into the Charles River if no one took her. However unintentionally, Inga was a living reminder of my ex.

I was going to brave my fears and get over this! I was twenty-six, for God's sake, and I was going to move on from this relationship with maturity. I sighed, stepped into the kitchen, and reached up to a high shelf to retrieve a few cookbooks. In case I got to interview for the job, I'd better be prepared. In the past, I'd leafed through cookbooks for recipes. Now, I looked at them as books. In particular, one thing that would be different about working on a cookbook from working on other written material would certainly be the formatting. Flipping through the pages of a Julia Child book, I saw that the number of servings was designated at the top and that the ingredients were listed in the order they were used. Abbreviations, I realized, all had to be consistent. I grabbed another book and then another and another. Some books had lovely forewords that informed the reader of the culinary delights that followed. Some books paired anecdotes with recipes, and some had glossy, mouthwatering photos. My stomach growled as I stared at a gorgeous crown roast of lamb, tied in a circle and filled with a creamy polenta and sausage stuffing. I slammed the book shut. I had nothing in my fridge except leftover pizza and flat seltzer water.

I took a shower, threw on a pair of sweatpants and an old T-shirt, and pulled my red hair into a ponytail. I understood all too well that my lack of a romantic life explained why I was putting no effort into doing my hair and makeup and picking out a cute outfit, but what did my appearance really matter today? It was Sunday, and I was just going to be lounging around my place doing homework. I dutifully gathered together my social work reading material and flopped down on the couch, determined to get through the seven dry chapters that lay ahead of me.

I read three chapters and then cringed at the title of the fourth: "Love and Attachment." Great! Exactly what I did not feel like reading about. In fact, the bane of my studies this fall had been this damn Attachment class. I threw the book across the room, shut my eyes, and willed my pain to retreat for a few hours.

Minutes later, when the phone rang, I gleefully snatched it from its cradle. Maybe it was Adrianna calling, and I could blow off my homework and go snuggle with baby Patrick. I didn't recognize the number on caller ID but picked up anyway. Even talking to the credit card company would be a welcome distraction.

"Hello?"

"Hi. I'm trying to reach Chloe Carter," a friendly male voice said.

"Speaking," I said with disappointment. A telemarketer?

Those people were always so goddamn friendly when they asked for you.

"Ms. Carter, this is Kyle Boucher." He pronounced his last name in the French manner: Boo-shay. "I put out the ad for a writing assistant."

"Oh! Yes!" I couldn't contain my excitement. "That was fast. I just sent my résumé a few hours ago. And please call me Chloe. Oh, have you already filled the position?" I knew I should have started job hunting sooner.

"Please call me Kyle. And, no, in fact, you're the first person to respond. I guess the idea of being a cookbook assistant didn't capture many people's interest. I was thrilled to find your résumé in my inbox."

"Really? That's great. It sounds like a job that I'd love."

"Excellent. Maybe we could set up an interview. In fact, why don't we. meet at a restaurant? Have you been to Oracle?" Kyle asked.

"No. That place opened about six months ago, right? I've heard good things about it." I'd been dying to go there, actually. Josh and I had managed to get a reservation one night last summer, but he'd had to cancel at the last minute when his boss at his old restaurant, Simmer, had insisted that Josh needed to work.

"Any chance that you're free to meet tomorrow night? Seven o'clock? I'm really behind on this project, and I'd love help as soon as possible." The hint of desperation in Kyle's voice raised my hopes for securing the job. "I've already made a reservation there for four, since I'd been hoping for a number of candidates to interview, but one enthusiastic response like yours is better than three wishy-washy ones."

"Perfect. I'll see you then. And thank you so much for calling."

When I hung up, I realized that for the first time since Josh had left, I was feeling truly upbeat and optimistic. It felt good to have something to look forward to. The only thing nagging at me was the prospect of going out to dinner with a strange man. Not that Kyle had sounded particularly *strange* on the phone, but dining at a restaurant with a man brought up images of an actual date, something I was nowhere near ready for. Stupid of me, I thought. This was a job interview. I hadn't met Kyle on a dating site, for Pete's sake. Still, I was suddenly nervous. For all I knew, Kyle was a psycho ax murderer, and posting ads for cookbook writers was his way of finding victims. Unlikely, I admit, but I nonetheless did what any other sensible, modern woman would have done: I searched Google Images for Kyle Boucher. After skipping over photos of men who certainly weren't my prospective employer—unless he was ninety-eight years old or a professional soccer player or a congressman—I located one shot of him. He looked normal enough, but in the picture he was in a group of people at a high school reunion, and I continued to feel wary. Sociopaths were always described as totally normal looking, and I wasn't in a mood to take risks right now. I called Adrianna.

She picked up after a few rings. "Spit-up and poop central. How can I help you?"

"Stop answering the phone like that," I complained. "It's so gross. Patrick does more than spit up and poop."

"True. He does occasionally sleep. Although not for more than four hours at a time. And he cries, too. It's charming."

Adrianna sounded beyond exhausted. Before Patrick's birth, Ade's knowledge of children in its entirety could have been handwritten in large print on a small index card. What's more, she'd never been one of those women who spend their lives dreaming about becoming mothers. On the contrary, she'd always had a rather strong dislike of children. Consequently, she'd reacted to finding out that she was pregnant with horror followed by panic. Fortunately, by the time Patrick had entered the world, she'd mellowed out, and some sort of instinctual parenting impulse had kicked in. Ade was hardly the soft, soothing motherly type, but Patrick was bringing out the best in the previously underdeveloped side of her. Besides, Owen was a fabulous father, and his enthusiasm had been contagious.

"But you know," she continued, "I wouldn't trade this little guy for anything. He giggles a lot now, too. Have you seen that? I got the cutest picture of him smiling. I'll send it to you later. So, what's up, Chloe? Are you coming over later? We miss Auntie!"

"I'm totally bogged down with homework for the rest of the day, but I wanted to see if you could come out to dinner with me tomorrow. Will Owen be home to stay with Patrick?"

"Yeah, Owen will be here, but I *cannot* afford to go out, you know that. And neither can you!"

"Actually, it's for a job interview." I explained the ad and the call from Kyle. "I don't think I should go alone."

"Chloe, you can't show up for a job interview with your best friend tagging along. It's not quite as bad as bringing your mommy, but close."

"Please! I'll pay for you, and it'll give you a good excuse to get out of the house for a few hours. We'll come up with an explanation for why you're there, and then I won't worry about being kidnapped after dessert."

Adrianna paused. The prospect of going out for a real meal had to be enticing. "Fine. But don't blame me if you end up embarrassed that you brought me. Oooh, what am I going to wear? And I'll get to do my hair and everything!"

"See? This'll be fun. I'll pick you up at six thirty tomorrow."

I was starting a new chapter in my life: a Josh-free chapter. Good!

Two

"HURRY up!" I pleaded with Adrianna. "You look as disgustingly gorgeous as you always do. I don't want to be late." Adrianna was in her bathroom touching up her eye makeup for the fiftieth time.

I stood in the doorway cradling Patrick in my arms. If I held this little bundle any longer, I might not want to leave. Ade had just nursed and burped him, changed his diaper, and dressed him in an adorable blue sleeper. I rubbed his peach fuzz with my finger and stared into his blue eyes. "Your mother is obsessing over perfection, isn't she?"

"We're not going to be late, Chloe. And this is practically the first time that I've gone out at night since I had the baby, and I want to look nice. There, this is as good as it's going to get, I guess." She spun around. As usual, I was taken aback by how beautiful my friend was. Her perfectly foiled blonde hair fell across her shoulders and down her back in soft curls, and even exhaustion couldn't detract from her modelesque face. Her body was heavier than it had been prepregnancy, but the little bit of extra weight only made her more curvaceous and attractive than ever. Breastfeeding had kept her cleavage annoyingly full. God, sometimes I hated standing next to her.

"You look too nice. With you there, Kyle won't be able to pay attention to any of my qualifications."

"Shut up," she said, waving her hand dismissively. "You look awesome."

Oracle was a pretty high-end restaurant, so I'd put on a sleeveless black dress that fell just above the knee and paired it with simple black pumps. With hair as red as mine, there's no need to add additional touches of color. I'd flat-ironed my curls until smoke had risen off my head, and then I'd slathered in defrizzing serum. It had taken me nearly thirty minutes to do my makeup because I'd been fussing over how much or how little made me look professional and competent.

"You ladies ready to go?" Owen called from the kitchen. "Or am I going to have to shove you out the door?"

We walked down the short hall, and I reluctantly passed Patrick over to his father. "Here you go. If this dinner wasn't about securing a job, I'd hold this kid all night."

"Go have fun. Although I still think it's weird that you're bringing a chaperone to an interview." Owen lifted Patrick high in the air, eliciting a smile from the baby. He kissed

14

Patrick's belly and then continued nuzzling his face into the baby's tummy. Patrick grabbed a fistful of Owen's hair and pulled.

"Don't let him do that," Adrianna said. "He'll lick his hands and get poisoning from your hair gel."

Ade's husband had taken to styling his black hair with gobs of gel. The result was alarming height and elaborate waves. Owen's wild hair matched his outgoing and even eccentric personality. I thought that it suited him perfectly. He was just as gorgeous as his new bride. I found his dreamy Irish looks to be quite handsome.

"Get out of here, ladies. Go have fun. Patrick and I are going to grill burgers for dinner. It's men's night here."

"Where are you going to grill?" I asked.

"Out on the fire escape."

"You are not!" Adrianna shrieked. "That is an old wooden fire escape, and one little spark from your decrepit grill could ignite the entire building! That teeny little area out there is not a porch, Owen. It's a safety feature. Or it was until you decided to make it hazardous."

I crossed the room and looked through the window on the back door at Owen's grilling area. There was barely room for two people to stand. "Yeah, I think it's illegal to grill on a fire escape."

"We're on the top floor of this house, so we're not blocking anyone's path out," Owen insisted. "Besides, it's the back of the house, so no one driving by could see me out there. And I can't imagine that our landlords downstairs would care. Anyhow, they're away for two weeks."

"Well, you better not grill after they get back," Ade said

sternly. "They're looking for any excuse to kick us out, so please don't hand deliver a reason for them to evict us."

"Why would they kick you out?" I asked. "You guys just moved in here four months ago."

Ade shrugged. "It seems that they just don't want to rent the third floor anymore. They've been using the first two floors, and they've decided that they really want to convert the whole house back to its original design and use the entire building for themselves. It's only the two of them, so I don't see why they need all the space, but I guess they have the money to do it. Unfortunately for them, we signed a one-year lease, so they're stuck with us until next July. Unless my husband gets us sent packing."

Owen shrugged. "Well, we could use more space, so maybe it wouldn't be a bad thing. You have to admit that we are totally cramped in here."

Adrianna nodded and sighed. "I know, but we practically just moved in, and I don't feel like moving again. But you're right. We barely fit into this place, and it's just going to get worse in a few months when Patrick starts to crawl. But for tonight, please be careful and don't burn the place down, okay?"

"Nothing is going to happen, Adrianna." Owen rolled his eyes at his wife's worrying. "It's a nothing little grill, and don't forget that yours truly was a Boy Scout. I'm an expert when it comes to fire safety. My son and I are bonding this evening, so leave us alone to do manly things like play with fire. And burp."

After reeling off endless baby-care instructions, Ade kissed Owen and Patrick, and then stood frozen at the front door, staring at her boys. "Are you sure you'll be okay? I won't be gone too long."

"I promise we'll be fine, babe. Please go out and have fun. You spend twenty-four hours a day with the baby. You deserve a few hours off, okay? I swear I'll call you if we need anything." Owen smiled reassuringly.

"Okay." She sighed again and didn't move.

"Ade, you're making me feel guilty. If you don't want to come, I understand," I said.

"No, she's going with you. Chloe, drag her down the stairs if you have to," Owen ordered.

"I'm going. I'm going. Bye," she said pathetically. "I love you guys."

"We love you, too. Bye, Mommy." Owen lifted Patrick's hand and waved his son's arm. "Have fun, Mommy."

"Oh no, Adrianna! You can't cry," I insisted. "Not after you spent all that time on your makeup!"

"Fine. Let's go." She rushed out the door, down the stairs, and into my car.

We drove in silence to the downtown restaurant. I knew that once I got her inside she'd relax. There was no way she'd be able to resist a good meal, and Oracle had been receiving glowing reviews in both local and national publications. For once, I sprang for valet parking. Tonight, I didn't want to waste time cruising Boston's jammed streets and risk finding nothing but an itty-bitty space that would require parallel-parking skills superior to mine. As I got out of the car, I felt self-confident. We were on time. I was going to make a good impression on Kyle Boucher. I was going to keep Ade from crying. Most of all, I was going to get this job.

THREE

FOR a Wednesday night, Oracle was crowded. I took its popularity as a sign that the food would be wonderful. The large dining area was almost entirely pale blue, as if the designer had wanted to create the feel of an artful house of ice: blue walls, blue linens on the tables, and even ice blue tile on the floor. The candles glowing from wall sconces and the miniature glass pendant lights hanging from the ceiling suggested a starry sky above the diners. It was magical! Better yet, contrary to appearances, the temperature was perfectly comfortable.

I approached the hostess stand. "I'm here to meet Kyle Boucher."

"Excellent. Your party is already seated. Right this way."

I followed the hostess to a corner of the restaurant, where a blond, goateed man in his early thirties sat alone. I recognized Kyle from his photograph, but he was much better looking than the small picture had indicated. He slid out of the semicircular booth and stood up. With a warm smile, he said, "You must be Chloe."

"And you must be Kyle." I shook his hand. "It's a pleasure to meet you. And this is my friend Adrianna." Uh-oh! I'd forgotten to come up with an explanation for her presence at dinner.

"Adrianna, it's lovely to meet you, too." Kyle showed no sign of finding it bizarre that a job applicant had turned up for her interview with a friend in tow.

"I hope you don't mind that I tagged along," Adrianna said apologetically. "I have a three-month-old baby, and I practically begged Chloe to bring me with her tonight. I just had to get out of the house." Talk about a true friend!

"I don't mind a bit. The more the merrier," he said graciously and gestured for us to take seats.

I scooted into the middle of the arched booth so that I sat between my friend and my potential boss. Kyle was indeed a good-looking man. Not that I cared, obviously, but he was tall, and his athletic build was visible even under his navy suit. His golden hair was neatly cut, but his goatee needed a trim. That slight hint of imperfection gave him a scruffy appeal.

The waitress appeared with our menus, and Kyle ordered a bottle of white wine for the table. Ade smirked at me, and I rolled my eyes. Since Patrick's birth, Adrianna had been out at night only once before, when I'd insisted that she accompany me to a local bar. In full-blown mourning for Josh, I'd gotten it into my head that nothing but a night of beer and tequila shots would heal me. According to Adrianna, the evening ended with my performing an atrociously morose rendition of "Son of a Preacher Man." On the walk home I capped the performance with a rather violent bout of vomiting. Perhaps I wouldn't drink much tonight. Just one glass. Or two, maybe.

"I guess I should start by telling you about the project I'm working on. Then you can decide if it sounds terrible or not. I won't be offended if you rush out of here before dessert," said Kyle, crinkling his eyes in a smile.

"If it has to do with food, I'm sure I'll love it," I said.

"Well, the cookbook I'm putting together is going to be a compilation of recipes from Boston chefs. My plan is to visit local restaurants, make sure the food is good, of course, and then solicit recipes from the chefs."

I immediately realized that Kyle's plan had a major problem—namely, the existence of cookbooks exactly like his, such as the popular *The Boston Chef's Table*. My job prospects seemed to be dwindling by the second. "Do you have a publisher lined up?"

My face must have shown my concern because Kyle said, "Yes, and don't worry. I know that there have been other Boston-based cookbooks, but this one's going to be part of a series of books with recipes from restaurants in major US cities. Boston is the first of the series, followed by LA, Chicago, Seattle, Atlanta, and Miami. My father is actually the name and the force behind the books. You may have heard of him. Hank Boucher?"

"Wow," I said, stunned.

"No way." Adrianna's mouth dropped open.

Hank Boucher was a nationally known chef who, according to all of the tabloid shows and entertainment magazines, catered everything from celebrity weddings to award-show parties. He was almost as well known as Wolfgang Puck or Mario Batali. I'd seen him on television and in magazines many times.

Kyle laughed lightly at our expressions. "So I gather you do know who he is. That's my father. And so the cookbook series is going to be his, with the titles including his name. This one will be *Chef Boucher's Favorite Recipes from Boston*. I really need help fast because I'm racing against a deadline. Then I'm off to LA to work on that book."

"Do you live in Boston?" I asked.

Kyle shook his head. "No, I'm just renting a small apartment near Boston Common. I've been in town for a few months already, but I haven't exactly gathered much material." He cleared his throat. "And, see, my dad is in France right now, but he'll be coming to Boston tomorrow to check on my progress, and . . . well . . ."

"You don't have anything to show him?" prompted Adrianna.

"Correct," he said sheepishly as he nodded at her. "That's where I hope Chloe will come in. But first things first. Let's order, shall we? If the food here is as good as it's rumored to be, Chloe might have her first assignment: soliciting the chef here for a recipe."

We opened our menus, and I read every delicious line. "It certainly looks incredible." Considering the exorbitant prices, it had better be. Well, I'd just charge the meal to my credit card and pray that Kyle hired me.

As if reading my thoughts, Kyle said, "Please order whatever you like. This is my treat, of course. In fact, order *more* than you like. We should taste as many dishes as we can so we can see which ones we might like for the book. And Adrianna," he said to my friend, "you especially should eat a lot, since you probably have no time to eat while taking care of a tiny baby, huh?"

Ade nodded. "That's very true. It's amazing how much time I spend holding Patrick, my son, rocking him, nursing, trying to get him to sleep. Not to mention doing the obscene amount of laundry the kid generates. Half the time I'm too tired to think about finding something to eat, never mind actually cooking anything. I'm usually in bed by eight o'clock, so forgive me if I nod off," she said jokingly. "The other mothers in my new-moms' group all say they do the same thing."

"I didn't know you went to a moms' group," I said. How could I not know? I knew everything about Adrianna!

"It's an online group. A discussion board, really, and we just post messages back and forth about what life is like with a new baby. I thought I'd told you. There are some really nice people on there, except that we are all so deliriously tired that our typing tends to be filled with typos and made-up abbreviations. Anyhow, Kyle, this really is a treat, so thank you again for letting me impose."

Kyle smiled kindly at her. "The more people we have to taste the food at Oracle, the better the book will be."

The server returned to take our orders, and Ade and I

insisted that Kyle choose for the table. The fall season meant that delicious upscale comfort food dominated the menu. I was looking forward to the pumpkin and apple bisque that came with caramelized apples and croutons, and there was a watermelon antipasto with prosciutto and fresh mozzarella that sounded unusual and fabulous. No one but a chef could get good watermelon in November. Especially in my all-but-bankrupt state, I envied chefs for being able to order any ingredients they wanted and charge everything to their restaurants.

Kyle reached under the table and retrieved a thick accordion folder that he passed to me. "I . . . um, well, this is what I have. I'm mortified that I have to show this to you, but I suppose you'd figure out how disorganized I am on your own anyhow." He shrugged. "You'll see why I'm in need of help."

I removed the elastic from the folder and found that it was jammed with scraps of paper, notes scrawled on the backs of old envelopes, and the occasional full-sized sheet of paper with handwritten recipes. Oh my. I took out a piece of yellow paper and saw a list of ingredients followed by illegible notes.

"Is that the one from Chez Marc?" Kyle peered at the paper. "Yes. At least I think it is. It's his recipe for roast chicken with something on the side. What does that say? Rots manageable? That can't be right."

"Root vegetables, maybe," I suggested.

"Yes!" Kyle said enthusiastically. "Root vegetables! The chef does the most amazing root vegetable puree that he flavors with cardamom."

"See?" Ade said. "Chloe is a natural."

Kyle smiled at her. "I think you're right. I better hire her, don't you think?" He turned to me. "What do you say? Has this folder of chaos scared you off?"

I laughed. "Not at all. I can get in touch with these chefs and have them clarify any confusion we have, and then I'll type everything up. Maybe we could get a little background on each chef? And have a short bio or an introduction of some sort for the recipe?"

"Perfect! I'll pay you by the hour, so just keep track of your time and give me a total at the end of each week." Kyle quoted me an hourly sum that was twice what I'd hoped for.

When our appetizers arrived, Adrianna practically inhaled her plate. "I had no idea how much I missed real food," she said with a sigh. "This lobster mac and cheese is unbelievable. Owen refuses to eat seafood at home since he's around it all day. Not that we can afford to be buying expensive fish fillets right now anyhow, but I'm pretty damn sick of eating plain chicken and pork chops, so this is such a luxury, Kyle."

Kyle laughed and smiled at my pal. "Please, it's nothing. So his work isn't going well? I'm sorry to hear that. And you at home with a young child? It sounds like things are tough right now."

Ade stuffed her mouth and nodded. God, she was really packing it in. Admittedly the food was excellent. My braised short ribs with hoisin sauce and wasabi mashed potatoes were outstanding. So was the watermelon appetizer. Who would've thought of this combination? But the sweet vinegar dressing went perfectly with the fruit, cheese, and meat. I was in heaven. But it seemed that Adrianna's ravenous appetite had erased her memory of table manners. I signaled to her to wipe her mouth.

She paused for air. "Yeah, he works hard as a seafood salesman, believe me, but I wouldn't complain if his paycheck was double what it is. At least he's had the same job for longer than a month. Progress, I suppose."

"Owen has a history of trying his hand at a . . . well, a varied set of careers," I explained.

"He's worked on a blimp, assisted a puppeteer, sold insurance," Adrianna said as she counted on her fingers. "You get the idea. So we're all pleased that he's trying to stick this one out and build up a solid set of customers. But you know how tough the restaurant business is. The restaurants struggle just like everyone else does. Sometimes they don't want to pay much above cost, so Owen ends up making pennies off of the product he sells. Plus, that damn refrigerated truck pisses through gas, and he's got to cover that himself."

I glared at Adrianna. How could she dare to say *pisses* during my interview?

"Would you like to work on the cookbook, too? You could make some extra money," Kyle offered.

"God no! I mean, thank you and all, but organizational skills are not my thing right now. I can barely keep my eyes open most of the time. I'm so tired that I'm putting dishes away in the freezer and ice cream in the cabinet. I throw clothes in the dryer and forget to turn it on, and then I can't figure out why they're still wet two hours later. Besides, Chloe will be really good for you, and I wouldn't want to mess that up."

"Let me know if you change your mind. I'm sure there'll be enough to do. So, Chloe, maybe you can start by seeing what you can make out of the mess in the folder. There's a list in there of restaurants my father wants me to approach, but the one we really have to deal with immediately is a place called Simmer. Do you know anything about that place?"

My stomach dropped. Simmer was Josh's restaurant, or rather, his former restaurant. He had slaved over helping to open Simmer last New Year's Eve and had routinely worked twelve-hour or even fourteen-hour days, often six days a week. He had given his all to that damn restaurant until the pressure and unreasonable demands from his cokehead boss, Gavin, had nearly made Josh crack. When the owner's drug problem hit an all-time high, pardon the pun, Gavin had been shipped off to rehab and had temporarily closed the restaurant. Josh's friend Digger took over as the executive chef for roughly two weeks before the owner closed the doors permanently and sold the place to a buyer who turned it into a high-end bakery. Josh's experience at Simmer was, I thought, the main reason that he'd run off to Hawaii.

My face must have turned ashen, because Adrianna nudged me under the table. Finally, she spoke. "Chloe knows all about Simmer. It was a wonderful restaurant that served some of the best food in Boston, but it closed a few months ago."

Kyle's face lit up. "Oh, Chloe, do you know the chef? Josh something, right? Do you know where he is now?"

I cleared my throat. "Um, I think he's in Hawaii."

"Damn." Kyle sighed. "My father ate at Simmer once last spring. He said that the food was outstanding. He had a fresh vegetable spring roll with mango sauce that he still talks about. It's the one restaurant that he insisted on. He said that it had to be in the book." Kyle pinched the bridge of his nose. "I really needed the chef for this project. My father is going to kill me. I probably shouldn't even be trying to make this whole thing happen." Kyle looked at us. "Sorry, I'm just really stressed out about my father's visit, as you can tell. He's not exactly the warm-and-fuzzy type."

I did have Josh's e-mail address, so technically I could get in touch with him. But it didn't seem right to have ignored all of his attempts to contact me and then suddenly write him a note to beg for a recipe. What could I say? *You broke my heart, and I've had to force myself out of bed every day, and I'm so mad at you and so hurt, and why did you leave me? And by the way, I need to know how to make your spring rolls.* Fat chance.

"A guy named Digger replaced Josh briefly before they closed, but I'm sure we can do something with the material you already have, Kyle." I tried to sound reassuring. "There's probably a lot more here in your folder than you think, and we'll get some more recipes before your father comes. He won't even notice that Josh's recipe isn't included."

Kyle managed a smile. "Believe me, he'll notice. He notices everything. Well, what about this Digger person that you said took over after Josh left? Do you know where he is?"

Ade shifted uncomfortably in her seat. Digger might have been and maybe still was Josh's good friend, but the details of how he'd taken over Josh's job had been a little sketchy. The sequence of his accepting the job and Josh's quitting was open to question, and even if Josh had resigned first, there was an unwritten rule in the restaurant world that banned moving in on another chef's territory the way Digger had. Josh had spent months complaining about how he was being treated at Simmer, and for Digger to move there with no hesitation suggested callousness about how beaten up Josh had been. But Josh had let it go. He and Digger had gone to culinary school together and had been close friends ever since. I was much more bothered by Digger's behavior than Josh was.

I hadn't seen Digger since Josh had taken off, but I had his phone number. As reluctant as I was to contact someone so close to Josh, I desperately needed a job, and this one was really perfect for me. "Yes, I know Digger. I'm sure he'd contribute some recipes for the cookbook. I'm not sure what restaurant he's at now, but he's a very skilled chef— excellent—so it's probably someplace you'll be glad to include."

Kyle brightened. "Do you think he'd have any recipes from Simmer?"

I shrugged. "Possibly. He wasn't there that long, but he might." As pissed as I was at Josh, I would never ask Digger for Josh's recipes, which belonged to Josh and not to Digger. Besides, chefs kept some recipes secret, so Josh might not have told even his good friend how to make some of his specialties. There was also Digger's pride to consider: although I hadn't quite forgiven him for taking Josh's job, I could hardly show more eagerness for Josh's recipes than for his own. When I talked to him, I'd need to be tactful.

"That would be fantastic! I'll e-mail my father and let

him know that we're working on a lead. It'll be better if he thinks this book is well underway, and I ought to be able to catch up before he gets to Boston."

"What's he doing in France?" I asked.

"Oh, supposedly he's traveling the country for research purposes. Learning new regional cuisines and all that. But mostly he's just showing off his latest trophy wife, Miranda. This is his fourth wife in the past eleven years. Once this most recent young wife shows the first sign of losing her looks, my father will drop her and move on. But for now, Dad is enjoying showing Miranda off, and I'm sure she's been paraded around at every possible European event." Kyle shook his head. "I couldn't tell you anything about this wife. I've given up trying to get to know any of them. They come and go so quickly that they've all blurred into one image for me. He's got a prototype that he fills every few years, so there's no point in my learning who's who. I don't know why he doesn't just pick one and stick with her."

When our entrées arrived, my mouth watered at the sight of my lamb. It smelled heavenly! The grilled lamb was served with cannellini beans and a rich salsa verde. The server who'd brought our main courses had pushed a rolling cart with preparations for Kyle's steak au poivre near our table. A sous-chef appeared and set a pan over an open flame. He then dropped a thick pepper-covered steak into the pan, causing billows of smoke to erupt.

"I love anything prepared tableside, don't you?" Kyle asked us as he stared happily at the sous-chef. "Wait until he lights the pan on fire. It's gorgeous!"

When the steak was done, the sous-chef removed it and

poured in a generous amount of pungent cognac. He tilted the pan and lit the cognac on fire, and the three of us almost involuntarily clapped our hands. It was like watching a show! When the fire subsided, the sous-chef added heavy cream to the sauce and then poured the rich concoction over Kyle's steak.

"That's great, isn't it? I go to those Japanese restaurants sometimes, the ones with the group tables where they do the hibachi cooking. I love it when the chefs make the onion volcanoes and fire shoots up from the onion rings. My father would probably faint if he knew I went to those kinds of restaurants, but I enjoy them." He sounded like an excited child talking about Disney World.

Ade nearly choked on her food, and I laughed. "We shouldn't talk about hibachis in front of her right now. Her husband is at home grilling on a small hibachi on their wooden fire escape."

"Yes, my idiot husband is probably going to burn our apartment down tonight. We don't have the money to buy a new grill, never mind to pay for rebuilding our apartment!" Ade flipped her blonde hair behind her shoulder and took a deep breath. "What am I going to do with him, huh?"

"Aw, it could be worse," I said. "Besides grilling outside, he could be trying to flambé things in the kitchen. Could you imagine him igniting cognac in the apartment?"

"Don't even suggest that!" she said. "If he hears about this steak tonight, then you know he'll want to replicate it at home. I'll have to keep the details of this delicious dinner a secret." She winked conspiratorially at us.

I worked my way through a plate of succulent lamb, and

by the time dessert arrived, Kyle and I had agreed that I'd keep his folder of notes so that his father, the famous Hank Boucher, wouldn't have the opportunity to see the mess of recipes and crumpled papers. Chef Boucher wouldn't see anything about the book until I had at least turned Kyle's notes into neat, tidy pages. Boy, did I have work ahead of me. I felt less guilty about accepting such a generous hourly rate now that I knew about the late nights that lay ahead of me.

I sampled the tiramisu and smiled. "Maybe we should get this recipe." I groaned. "It's sinful!" Tiramisu was one of those desserts that could be either outstanding or totally mediocre. This one, with its layers of mascarpone, liquor-soaked ladyfingers, and cocoa, was rich and decadent.

"So, Chloe, not to rush you too much, but do you think you could contact this Digger character tomorrow and see what Simmer recipes you can get your hands on?"

"Sure. No problem."

"It's just that with my father coming into town tomorrow, I'd really like to do what I can to avoid a fight. I know I can get this book together and really impress him, but I think it'd be best to make a strong first presentation."

"Absolutely. I'll get in touch with you as soon as I speak to Digger," I assured my new boss.

After we had thoroughly gorged ourselves on dinner, Kyle paid the bill and left a substantial cash tip. "If you'll excuse me, I think I'm going to ingratiate myself with the chef and see if I can finagle a recipe or two and an interview from him. Thank you so much, Chloe, for taking this on. And, Adrianna, it was a delight to meet you. I hope to see you both again soon." He shook our hands and headed off toward the rear of the restaurant.

Ade helped herself to the last bite of my dessert. "So, Chloe," she said, "good work. Not only did you find yourself a great job, you also just found a potential husband."

"What?" I said with irritation. "That man is not husband material. He's my employer. We are going to have a strictly professional relationship."

"We'll see," she said in a singsong voice. "I think he is adorable and charming and sweet. Maybe this is a sign that it's time to move on?"

Move on. I'd love to move on, except that I was about to dig myself back into Josh's culinary world by calling Digger and asking for Simmer recipes. My new job was going to make it harder than ever to shake Josh out of my system.

Four

I spent Thursday at my internship, or "field placement" as my graduate school referred to it, at a community mental health center where I provided counseling services to an array of clients. Draining though those days were, they kept my mind from wandering to my romantic troubles. When I returned home, my car slid on wet leaves as I pulled into my parking spot by my condo. November weather stank. It was freezing, with bitter winds and gray skies dominating the forecast for the next ten days. Now, at four fifteen or so, it was already as black as midnight, and I was missing spring terribly. I walked up to my third-floor condo and immediately turned on all the lights and lit a few sugar-scented candles. I was fighting the urge to get into bed and hide, but

I was determined to beat this endless Josh hangover. Last night's conversation about Simmer had stirred up memories of my frequent visits to see Josh at work, the way he looked after a long night in the kitchen, how his once-white chef's coat would be all dirty and smelly but somehow comforting. His hair would be mussed up and adorable, and his blue eyes were always filled with exhaustion. . . . I had to stop! I refused to let this gloomy day bring me down. My interesting new job would eat up a lot of the time that I'd otherwise have spent lolling around, pining over my chef. No, I corrected myself, not *my* chef. A chef. Just one more chef. No one special.

I scooped up one of my cats, Inga, and nuzzled her white fur. She'd been terribly scrawny when I'd first taken her in, but she'd gained weight. I was, however, still struggling to keep up with her constant need for thorough grooming. These days, she got the occasional knot and was nowhere close to the matted mess she'd been when Josh had rescued her. I loved having her and loved what a snuggler she'd become. Gato, my shorthaired black cat, was still pissed off that he was no longer an only feline. I frequently came home to rolls of shredded toilet paper that he'd left for me in the bathroom. Gato didn't fight with Inga, but he clearly had no interest in becoming kitty pals with her, either.

I had no idea what days Digger was off work, or even where he worked, but I decided to give him a call and at least leave him a message. I still had his cell number programmed into my phone, so I flopped onto my bed and dialed.

"Hello?" A woman answered his phone.

"Hi, this is Chloe. Is Digger there?"

"Chloe who? Who are you? What is this about?" she asked suspiciously. "Do I know you?"

Who was this girl, and why was she so rude? "I'm a friend of his. I wanted to talk to him about recipes."

"Oh, Chloe, right! I've heard about you. You used to go out with a friend of Digger's, right?"

I sighed. "Yes."

"Oh, okay. Good. I'm Digger's girlfriend, Ellie. Digger's working tonight, but you're interested in recipes? What do you need?"

I explained about Kyle's cookbook project and emphasized the name Hank Boucher. "I'm sure Digger knows who Hank is. Do you think he'd be interested? What restaurant is he at now?"

"He'll definitely be interested. Are you kidding?" she said enthusiastically. "He's about to be the executive chef at the Penthouse. It's a new, ultra-high-end place that's opening in a few weeks. I can't believe he got the job. Well, I can believe it because he's so talented, but the competition was crazy. You know how it is with chefs, though, right?"

"Yes, I do." In fact, I knew all too well. Chefs were often wildly passionate about their careers, and good jobs were hard to come by. The testosterone-fueled atmosphere of the restaurant kitchen, combined with the frenetic pace of cooking, gave rise to lots of cursing and hazing. Over the past year, Josh had regaled me with countless kitchen-insider stories. I knew more than I cared to about the politics of the restaurant world. Most of what went on in the industry was entirely crazy: endless power struggles among the waitstaff, the kitchen crew, the managers, and the owner. I was tuckered out just thinking about it.

"Anyhow," Ellie said, "the chef that Digger beat out for the job is totally pissed off, as you can imagine. I do have to take some credit, though, for my guy snagging this job. All the big-name chefs like Hank Boucher have managers, right? So I took it upon myself to act as Digger's manager and agent. It puts him in a more powerful light if I call up and schedule his interviews. I've been helping him direct his career and position himself to become a major player in the Boston chef circle."

Ellie sounded more than a little proud of herself. I, however, found her role ridiculous. Yes, nationally known chefs had managers and agents, but those celebrity chefs actually needed people to organize their schedules, make travel arrangements, set up interviews and television appearances, and do general PR. Digger, on the other hand, simply did not need a manager! He was a great chef, but he was by no means a household name. Furthermore, he was the last person on earth who'd enjoy being managed by anyone. He was loud, crass, direct, and confident, and as much as he might have wanted to get a great job, he didn't strike me as ambitious for the kind of fame and fortune that Ellie seemed to have in mind. He just loved being a chef and didn't need the spotlight on him to keep loving his work. I couldn't believe that he liked having his girlfriend take over his career.

"That all sounds great," I lied. "What type of food is he planning on doing at the Penthouse?"

"He's still working on the menu and trying out recipes, but he should have that all finalized soon. I have an idea.

Why don't you bring this cookbook guy, Kyle, to meet with Digger and sample some of the dishes he's working on?"

"That would be wonderful. I'd love to see him again, too. Where is the restaurant?" I asked.

"Unfortunately, it's not ready. They're still installing the new equipment and painting. Digger has been doing everything here, from his apartment. I'd let him use mine, but my kitchen is even smaller than his, so you two would have to come here."

I was disappointed that I couldn't take Kyle to a more impressive setting than Digger's home kitchen for our first collaboration. Young chefs like Digger, even at high-end restaurants, earned low salaries; they made far less than the servers did. He probably lived in a cheap apartment. His kitchen was sure to be old, small, and ugly, but it would have to do. Besides, I knew that his food would speak for itself no matter where we were, and Hank would never have to know that his son had sampled Digger's food in a crummy apartment rather than in a luxurious dining establishment. Once the Penthouse opened, Kyle and I could go there for the full experience.

"That sounds fine. Do you know when he'll be free?" I asked. Ellie was, after all, Digger's manager, or so she said. Maybe she was entitled to pencil us in.

"I'm sure that Digger will want to talk to you himself since you're a friend. But let me give you all of my contact information so you'll have it for later." Ellie began reeling off cell and fax numbers, e-mail addresses, and the best hours to reach her. "And now let me get your number and address so that I make sure you get an invitation to opening night."

As I dutifully dictated my information, I wondered whether the Penthouse's owner knew that Ellie was taking it upon herself to invite people to the restaurant's big night. "Thanks so much for your help," I said. "It was nice to talk to you. And I hope I'll meet you soon."

"Of course. I'll see if I'm free to be there when Digger cooks for you and Kyle. It'll be like a double date!"

"Kyle is—" I was on the verge of explaining that Kyle and I had a strictly professional relationship but then thought better of it. What did I care if Digger and Ellie thought that we were dating? And if word got back to Josh that I was seeing someone, then fine! Let him stew on that one. "Sounds great."

"I'll page Digger right now and have him get in touch with you. Bye, Chloe."

I hung up the phone. It was obvious that Ellie was enthusiastic about Digger and his career, but she sounded like a strange match for Digger, too bubbly and positive for the sarcastic, pessimistic, tough chef. But what did I know about love?

I was foraging in the fridge for the makings of dinner when the phone rang.

"Chloe!" Digger shouted at me. "What's up, babe?"

"That was fast," I said with a laugh.

"Yeah, my girl has me on a short leash. She just called me and instructed me to call you immediately. She says you have a PR opportunity for me, and I'd better get my ass in gear and get ahold of you." Metallic noises echoed through the phone so loudly that I had to pull the receiver away from my ear.

"Where are you? What is that racket?" I asked.

"Sorry. I'm at the restaurant tonight, and they're trying to get the new stoves in here. It's a goddamn nightmare. Christ, this sucks. Hold on. I have to stop these guys." Digger began yelling and cursing in his usual colorful manner and ended with, "How do you jackasses think you're going to move that stove in when you haven't taken the other one out yet? Evolution in reverse, right here, huh? Sorry, Chloe. So what's up?"

I quickly described Kyle's project. "So, do you think we could meet up with you to taste some recipes? Maybe do a short interview?"

"Did you even turn the frickin' gas off, you morons?" Digger screamed. "Chloe, I don't know. I'm mobbed here these days."

"Please? It's Hank Boucher's book, after all. How could you not want to be in that?"

The chef said something that I couldn't hear because of the banging in the background, but I did catch him saying, "How about Saturday morning? Ten o'clock at my place."

"Awesome. Thanks so much. It'll be good to see you."

I scrawled down the address he gave me. Just before I hung up, Digger let loose a stream of four-letter words. I smiled. I missed that guy. As crass as he could be, he had a wonderful heart and a gooey soft spot that I adored. I'd last seen Digger in August, when Josh and I had gone out to dinner at a Brookline restaurant, but I could tell that Digger hadn't changed.

There was Josh, creeping into my thoughts again. Instead of distracting myself with dinner, schoolwork, or television,

I went into the bedroom and pulled a thick scrapbook from a shelf. I crawled onto the bed and lost myself in the pages. I'd been putting the scrapbook together to give to Josh as an anniversary present. I'd saved cards he'd given me, movie ticket stubs, takeout menus from our favorite places, pictures of the two of us, and lots of other memorabilia. The pages went on and on. Well, I rationalized, I was doing well most of the time, wasn't I? Yes. So I was entitled to a night of misery here and there. I ran my finger over a picture of my chef. I missed that gorgeous face. I missed everything about him. Even so, I had blocked his e-mails and had changed my cell number after he'd kept leaving me messages. I didn't want to read his words or hear his voice. I couldn't. Why? Because as furious and confused as I was by his abrupt departure for Hawaii, I still loved him. Crap. I threw the book onto the floor and covered my eyes with my hands. I inhaled and exhaled deeply a few times, willing myself not to fall apart.

I sat up and shook my head. I had work to do! I took my laptop and Kyle's folder off the desk in my bedroom and carried everything to the living room, where I sat on the floor and spread the mess of notes on the coffee table. I spent an hour categorizing the papers: recipes for appetizers, soups, salads, poultry, meat, seafood, and dessert. Kyle had a number of lists, all full of ideas for chefs to contact, restaurants to look into, questions to ask chefs for biographies and interviews. He included suggestions for where pictures of the chefs could be taken and noted that the chef from Triba had a very attractive wife. Maybe they could be photographed together? I rolled my eyes. It took me over an hour to make a dent in the disastrous heap. Kyle wasn't kidding when he'd said that he needed help! I typed up six recipes, saved the file, and shut down the computer.

I decided to give Kyle a quick call to let him know we could meet up with Digger.

"Hello, Kyle? This is Chloe."

"Ah, Ms. Carter. This is Hank Boucher, here. My son said you might be calling."

Oh my God! I was talking to *the* Hank Boucher. I'd seen this man countless times on TV and in print, but actually to be talking to him right now? How cool! I'd have bet anything that he was about to invite me out to a fabulously expensive restaurant, too. L'espalier, maybe? I'd kill to go there.

"Mr. Boucher! Oh . . . it's an honor," I stammered foolishly.

"I understand you're my son's typist, correct? Have you finished?" he asked sternly.

Typist? I was more than a typist! Famous chef or not, Hank was not going to refer to me as a typist. "Actually," I said with annoyance, "I am assisting Kyle with the research angle of the book."

"Sure, sure. Sorry. What is that secretaries want to be called these days? How about *administrative assistant*? Is that better for you, dear?"

Oh, I got it: Hank Boucher was an asshole. The realization was more than a little disappointing.

I cleared my throat. "I've been able to arrange a meeting with one of the chefs from Simmer, Digger. He's about to open a very upscale restaurant called the Penthouse. He's agreed to share some of his recipes for the book, and we can sample some of the dishes that he's trying out for the new restaurant. Will you be joining us? Saturday morning at ten."

"Certainly. Where is this restaurant located?"

"Actually, we're meeting at the chef's apartment, because the restaurant is in the middle of construction right now."

"An apartment?" Hank made no attempt to hide his disdain. "Lord, where is this place?"

Hank Boucher and I were destined not to be the best of friends. I gave him Digger's address, which was in Somerville. I was beginning to hope that Digger's apartment was as tiny and shabby as I'd been assuming. Let Hank Boucher see how most chefs lived! Kyle would probably freak out when he learned that he was to take his father to a less-than-four-star location, but tough for him. For me, Saturday's gathering would be interesting. I looked forward to seeing how the celebrity chef would handle himself in the kind of home kitchen that a working chef could afford. Still, I cautioned myself to be pleasant. Hank Boucher's name was, after all, what would be selling the cookbook.

"It will be wonderful to meet you, Mr. Boucher. I've been a fan of yours for a long time and—"

"Chloe? Hi, it's me." Hank had obviously passed me off to Kyle. "What's going on?"

When I'd filled him in, he agreed that we'd all meet at Digger's place at ten. "Good job. I really appreciate your hard work. I can't wait to see you again."

I said good-bye. So Kyle couldn't wait to see me again, huh? In that case, I'd have to spend some time choosing my outfit for Saturday morning.

FIVE

I watched the steam float off of my head as I flat-ironed my hair. I was not going to let Kyle see me with frizzy hair, that was for sure! And it wouldn't hurt to have Digger see me looking polished, glamorous, and stable, either. Digger was undoubtedly in touch with Josh, and I wanted him to report to my ex that I was looking fabulous. In truth, I half wanted to throw on jeans and a sweatshirt and toss my hair in a ponytail, but I knew that it was good for me to have a reason to get up early and pull myself together this Saturday morning. I chose a stretchy button-down patterned shirt that I'd bought on sale at Ann Taylor Loft. I paired it with form-fitting black pants and tall black boots. Checking myself out in the full-length mirror, I was pleased to see that the pants were much more flattering than they'd been when my chef was feeding me all the time. Hah! Take that, Josh!

I left the house at nine and drove to Somerville. I'd realized the previous night that, as much as I wanted Hank Boucher to see how real chefs lived, I also didn't want him walking into a truly revolting apartment. Because chefs were rarely at home, there was an excellent chance that Digger's place desperately needed a good cleaning. His kitchen would be sanitary, but it might well be as messy as it was sterile. Granted, Digger's girlfriend, Ellie, could have taken over civilizing his apartment the way she'd taken over promoting his career, but I didn't want to risk it. Crummy equipment and small spaces were one thing, but a chaotic, neglected apartment would reflect badly on me, and I didn't want to give Hank any reason to fire me. Consequently, in case I needed to tidy Digger's apartment before Hank and Kyle Boucher arrived, I intended to get there early.

I checked my Google Maps printout as I scanned side roads for the turn to Digger's. Spotting the sign, I made a left onto a long street filled with three-decker apartment buildings, but before I was anywhere near Digger's address, I was forced to stop. Peering around a big van in front of me, I could see that, beginning a few blocks up, the street had been totally blocked off. Who did street work on a Saturday morning? And where were the detour signs? How annoying! And was it really necessary to stop all traffic? Lights flashed down the street, and a few cars had stopped close to some sort of barricade. Even without this mess, it would've been hard enough to park around here with three-deckers smack-dab one right after another, each jammed with tenants. I growled and pulled my car to the right, into a minuscule parking place, a permit-only spot for residents, but what choice did I have? I'd get a visitor permit from Digger, or I'd take the ticket. Didn't the Somerville parking honchos know that I had important work to do? Men to impress? Baby-supply bills to pay off? I got out of the car, slammed the door, swung my tote bag over my shoulder, and hit the lock button on my remote.

Then the smell hit me. Smoke.

I whipped my head toward the stopped cars ahead of me and scanned the area. The flashing lights weren't coming from construction vehicles but from a fire engine. I rushed along the sidewalk until I reached what turned out to be a police barricade, where a number of people were milling around, murmuring and shaking their heads. Across the street from where I stood were the remains of a three-decker, the outside charred black, the windows smashed in, the ugly shell drenched in water. The horrendous stench of wet, charred wood filled the air. Foul, filthy water lay in puddles in the street. I clapped my hand over my nose and looked down at the scrap of paper in my hand, the one with Digger's address. His house was number 432. I glanced up. To the left of the ruined building was number 430. I scrambled ahead a few steps and looked at the building to the right of the burned-out three-decker: 434.

The fire had been in Digger's building. Worse, according to the directions I'd been given, his apartment was on the ground floor, the blackest and most hideously damaged section of the building. It didn't take a fire investigator to see that the back of the building was the hardest hit. My heart raced. Nearby, a small crowd had gathered around a police officer who stood just beyond a strip of yellow police tape that marked off the area in front of Digger's building. I scanned for Digger but couldn't see him anywhere. His absence meant nothing, I assured myself. Digger was a big, strong, tough dude, I told myself. Digger was just fine.

"What happened here?" I asked a young woman next to me. "When did this happen?"

She bit her cheek. I could see that she had been crying. "Early this morning. I live there. Or used to live there. We've been out here for hours, waiting until they let us go back in and salvage what we can. They gave us these blankets, and at least it isn't freezing today, but I don't know where to go. I don't have anyone." She ran a hand through her short hair. Her fingers trembled. "It's just awful. Someone died. Someone died!" she repeated more loudly before dropping her head.

It simply couldn't be Digger. It just *couldn't*. "Who?" I asked as calmly as I could.

"I'll tell you who died," grumbled a short, plump man in his late forties. He looked exhausted, but he also looked incredibly irritated. I, in turn, felt irritated with him. A tragic fire was a cause for sadness, fear, stress, and grief. But irritation?

I glared at him. "Do you live here, too?" I asked.

He frowned. "Thank God, no. I don't know if the building is even livable anymore after what that stupid moron did to the place. I mean, look at it!" He pointed angrily to the building. "I live right next door, and it's the last time I ever live near a goddamn chef, that's for sure. I'm lucky he didn't burn down my place, too, since I'm right next to him."

I froze. "Did you say *chef*?"

"Yeah, that's right. Frankly, he got what he deserved. He started the fire and got himself killed."

I started to panic. Okay, I told myself, Digger is not the only chef in Boston. Far from it! Boston is so flooded with restaurants that there could practically be one chef per building, couldn't there? Or maybe this guy meant *chef* in the casual sense—in other words, an enthusiastic amateur cook who thought of himself as a chef.

"What's your name?" I asked the man.

"Norris." He crossed his arms and rested them on his potbelly.

"Norris, I'm Chloe. How do you know it was a chef? What do you mean it was his fault?"

"That's his apartment," he said, pointing to the damaged first-floor unit. "That stupid chef was cooking all the time, day and night, and stinking up the whole neighborhood. He didn't care that my apartment smelled like fish or onions or whatever, but with me on the first floor right next door, he should've known that those nasty smells were going to seep into my place, right? He didn't care." Norris stroked his full beard and shook his head. "Jerk. There's what? Ten feet between these buildings? He could have killed me!"

Digger could have spent the night at Ellie's, right? In fact, if Ellie was like most other women, she wouldn't want to stay at a boy's icky apartment, especially a chef's. I'd slept at Josh's place only a handful of times when we were dating. Digger must have discovered the disaster when he'd arrived home this morning. Now, he was milling around here some-where. Or maybe Digger had a roommate who was also a chef? I dug my purse out of my bag and called Digger's cell. While it rang, I listened and glanced around, hoping to hear a phone ring, but I got Digger's voice mail and hung up. Okay, maybe Digger had had a friend staying with him. A terrible idea hit me: what if Josh had come to visit him and had been sleeping on his couch?

I approached the police officer. "Sir! Can you help me? I was supposed to meet someone who lives in that building. Can you please tell me who was killed in the fire?"

"Ma'am, I'm sorry. There hasn't been a formal identification yet. He was someone who lived here." The officer adjusted his hat and pulled his gloves on tighter.

"How can you not know who it is yet?" I paused. "Oh God." The dreadful image of an incinerated body, a body burned beyond identification, flashed through my head. What a monstrous way to die! "It must have been so awful . . . for . . ."

"We don't know much at this point, but I can tell you that it appears the victim died of smoke inhalation." He cleared his throat. "The guy was probably asleep and just never woke up. It looks like the fire started in the kitchen, probably at the stove, and the smoke detectors had been disabled. People do that sometimes, you know, if something has set them off, and then they just leave them that way. So it looks like this was all a terrible accident."

Oh no. Disabling the smoke detectors was just the sort of thing Digger would do, especially if he'd been doing a lot of cooking for the new restaurant. Chefs were used to big flames and lots of smoke while they cooked. After repeatedly setting off the smoke alarms, he'd probably gotten sick of opening the windows and fanning the rooms to get the noise to stop; I could easily picture Digger yanking the damn alarm out of the ceiling just to get it to shut up. But it looked like there were two apartments on the first floor, so maybe the fire hadn't started at Digger's place. I asked the officer.

He shook his head. "Thankfully the other person who lived downstairs is away for the week."

"That's right," Norris barked. "She went to Arizona. Joked she was excited to get away from the smell of ginger and coriander for a while. For me, that goddamn grease smell was the worst. Like we live at a McDonald's, for Christ's sake! In fact, grease is probably what started the fire. Grease fires are the worst, you know."

My knees began to buckle under as the reality of Digger's death hit me. I shot Norris a look. "That was my friend who died in the fire, you jerk. And his food wasn't greasy, ever! He was a talented professional chef, not some hack who did nothing but plunge frozen foods into a fryolator." My eyes began to sting, and I could hear my voice tremble.

"She's right." I felt a gentle hand on my back and looked to my right. A woman with graying hair pulled into a braid stood next to me. "That young man was a lovely person. He was sweet. He used to bring me food when he'd made extra, which happened a lot recently. He said he was working on a menu for a new restaurant, so he was cooking all the time, that boy. Yes, Norris, some of his food was sometimes a little peculiar, I'll give you that. He loved funny spices and strange vegetables that I'd never heard of, but that boy never made anything greasy, that's for sure. You watch your mouth, Norris, and don't speak ill of the dead," she warned.

Dead. My stomach twisted into a solid knot, and I dropped my head down between my knees to keep the world from spinning. I inhaled deeply, but all I took in was the rank smell of burned air. I stood up and managed a weak smile at the kind woman.

She nodded slightly at me and pulled a blanket tightly around her shoulders. "I'm Barbara. I lived upstairs. Chef Digger cooked for a living. He'd know all about kitchen fires. Norris, you know as well as I do that he'd be the last person to start one. Something else started that fire." She coughed. "Or some*one* else."

I froze and stared at Barbara. She was right. Even if Digger had been stupid enough to disable the smoke detectors, he was too skilled and too careful to cause a fire. He was just as fastidious as Josh was about keeping kitchens sanitary. Chefs were accustomed to unannounced visits from health inspectors and were keenly aware that inspection scores could affect their salaries and bonuses. Besides, Digger prided himself on maintaining a sterile kitchen. Even if the rest of his apartment had been a complete dump, there was no way that his kitchen would have had the layers of smelly grease and gunk that posed a fire hazard. He wouldn't have left an oven or burner on, of course. And if he had actually been cooking in the wee hours of the night and had somehow managed to start a fire, he certainly would have known how to put it out; he and Josh both kept bins of baking soda near their restaurant stoves so that they could dust out flames in an emergency. I'd have bet anything that Digger did the same at home.

A car horn blared. Turning, I saw a black Hummer idling in back of the police barricade. The driver was arguing with an officer. Until that moment, I'd totally forgotten about Kyle and Hank Boucher.

"Excuse me," I said to Barbara and Norris.

I made my way to the environmentally unfriendly vehicle that Hank had no doubt rented for his stay in Boston. I couldn't imagine that Kyle had chosen this monstrosity. My guess about who'd picked the Hummer spoke well for Kyle. In any case, his father was in the driver's seat—yes, probably in every sense of the phrase. Hank was just as well groomed off camera as he was on. He was a tall, lean man with graying hair that was slicked back, creating a severe look that I found unpleasant. I wondered if his deeply tanned skin was the result of his worldwide traveling or if it was one of those spray tans that were so popular with celebrities.

I approached the passenger's side of the Hummer as Hank was complaining about the neighborhood. "Nice work, son. You've managed to put us smack in the middle of luxury here, haven't you?" Hank gestured grandly. "We're sure to find culinary greatness living in one of these stupendous buildings. And just because there's a serious police presence in the neighborhood doesn't mean that we should be thwarted by the threat of gang violence, does it? Where the hell are we supposed to park around here, anyway? Not that I'm overly anxious now to get going with this supposed tasting you've set up, but since we're here, we might as well get it over with. I don't imagine there's valet parking nearby, is there?"

Kyle squirmed uncomfortably.

I pursed my lips. "Hello, Mr. Boucher," I said coldly. "I'm Chloe Carter. I hardly think you need to worry about gang violence or valet parking right now. There's been a fire in my friend Digger's building. He apparently died in the fire."

"Typical!" Hank barked angrily. His face barely moved, and I suspected a good dose of Botox was preventing any expression. "Good job, Kyle. This book is coming along swimmingly, isn't it?"

"Dad!" Kyle glared at his father. "You can't blame me for this."

"Christ, let's get out of this hellhole before something else happens." Hank started to back the car up to make a three-point turn.

Kyle shot me an apologetic look. "I'll call you later, Chloe."

I watched in disbelief as the pair drove off. Hank had hardly glanced at me, and Kyle had been too wrapped up in his father's obnoxious behavior even to ask how I was. I wanted to get out of there, too, but as I began to head toward my car, I realized that Digger's girlfriend and manager, Ellie, might not know of his death. Backtracking, I found Norris and Barbara still staring at the charred, sopping remains of the building.

"Does either of you know whether Digger's girlfriend has been here? Whether she knows what happened?" I asked.

Barbara shook her head. "Sorry, hon, I don't know anything about a girlfriend."

Norris rolled his eyes. "There's another thing. Not only did this guy smell up the entire street, but there was a whole business of women in and out of the place. Like we're some sort of brothel here!"

Before I could ask Norris what in the world he was talking about, a young man chimed in. "I live in the building. Or I did. And I know who you're talking about." He pulled a hat down over his ears. "She hasn't been here this morning. I've been out here since the fire, and I haven't seen her."

I thanked him and took off. On the way to my car, I imagined Ellie hearing about the fire on the radio or innocently turning on the television and seeing the blackened ruins of her boyfriend's apartment. I had to get to her first. I called her from my cell phone as I started my car.

She picked up almost immediately. "Yes? Chloe, is that you? Are you at Digger's?"

"Sort of. Ellie, I need to come see you right away."

"Is something wrong? I've been calling him all morning about the meeting with Hank Boucher. He decided he didn't want me there, if you can believe it, because his kitchen is so small. Did he screw something up?" she demanded.

"Not exactly, no. Ellie, I really need to come and talk to you. What's your address?"

Ellie paused. "Okay. I'm in Cambridge, not too far from Harvard Square." She gave me her street address and hung up.

A trip down Mass. Ave. followed by a few turns would get me to her place in no time. Despite the cold, I rolled down the window, and as I drove, I took gulps of fresh air. Of the many things that were upsetting me, what stood out most was something Barbara had said: her suggestion that someone else besides Digger could have started the fire. What if the fire hadn't been an accident, but arson? What if his death had been murder? But who on earth would want to kill Digger? Was Norris so fed up with the chef that he'd burned down the building, even at the risk of destroying his own apartment? Maybe Ellie would have some idea.

Six

ELLIE lived in half of a gorgeous old two-family house on a charming side street. To live in this part of Cambridge, right in the midst of Harvard University territory, she had to have money.

Announcing a boyfriend's death was not how I'd normally choose to meet someone. I had no idea what to say. In fact, all I could think of was what not to say. *Hi, nice to meet you. Your boyfriend is dead. Beautiful apartment, by the way. What's the rent like?*

When I rang the bell, Ellie called for me to come in. I pushed open the heavy front door and stepped into the living room, where a roaring fire heated the cozy room.

"Chloe." Ellie smiled as she emerged from a doorway.

"It's great to meet you. Come in and grab a seat. Would you like some coffee?"

"No, thank you. Um, Ellie . . ."

I stared at the young woman, who looked perky and chipper and incredibly voluptuous—big hair and big boobs. Her bouncy chestnut hair fell just below her shoulders, and her crisp clothes hugged her shapely curves.

I said, "You need to sit down." I nodded at the cream love seat by the fireplace.

"I knew something happened! Don't tell me Digger blew off Hank Boucher, of all people!" Ellie sat neatly on the cushion and crossed her legs. "If Digger would just listen to me, then he would have his own line of cookware by now. What am I going to do with him?"

"Ellie, there's been . . . I have something terrible to tell you. There is no easy way to say this, but . . ." I simply couldn't get the words out. I stared at her dark red lips, momentarily entranced by the thick layer of lipstick. "Last night . . . Digger . . ."

Ellie's face darkened as she listened to me struggle. "What is it? What is it?" Panic crept into her voice.

I had to spit it out. "There was a horrible fire at Digger's place last night. He died. No one has confirmed it yet, but I know that it was a chef who lived on the first floor of his building. It's obviously him."

Ellie threw her hands over her face and held still. Feeling hopelessly inadequate, I waited for her to fall apart. Her shoulders began to tremble, and tears soon leaked from behind her hands as she moaned and sobbed. I moved to sit next to her. Resting my hand on her back, I said, "I'm terribly sorry." I wiped my own cheeks. "This is such a tremendous shock. I can hardly believe it myself. I don't know what to say."

Ellie finally dropped her hands from her face. She looked positively heartbroken and miserable. Having no idea what to say, I reached out and wiped the mess of black mascara that ran down her face.

"How could this have happened?" she asked. "Why? And he was just about to really make something of himself. He was finally going to have his talent recognized! It's not fair! Do you have any idea what the competition for this new job was like? He was so proud of himself for beating out the other chefs. Rightfully so, too, because he was up against some very good chefs. This just isn't right!" She dropped her head, crying hard.

I snatched a handful of tissues from an end table and handed her the pile. "Can I call someone for you?" Ellie, I thought, needed the presence of someone she was close to, a friend or a family member, not the stranger who had delivered the devastating news.

"Georgie," she said through her tears. "Call Georgie. My phone . . ." She pointed to a purse that sat by the front door.

I scrambled for her purse and found her cell phone. A quick scroll down through her contacts, past a list of numbers for Digger, revealed Georgie. I called the number and was relieved when Georgie answered immediately. I explained who I was and asked her to come to Ellie's as soon as possible. Although I didn't tell her about Digger, she must have caught the gravity of my request, because she assured me that she'd be right over. As we waited, I did what I could to comfort Ellie. My ineffectual efforts consisted mainly of emptying the box of tissues and murmuring words of condolence until the front door finally burst open.

"What's wrong?" A tall, thin waif of a woman stood in front of us, her short blonde hair tucked behind her ears. "Ellie?" she asked with concern as she knelt in front of her friend.

"Digger is dead," Ellie managed to whisper. "There was a fire and he's dead!" More tears followed, of course, and more tissues.

Georgie's already fair skin paled as she crumpled to the floor, holding herself up with her hands. "Oh my God. No! No!" She burst into choked sobs. "Oh, Digger! No!"

I shut my eyes for a moment. The grief was so painful to witness that I knew I'd be unable to hold myself together much longer. At least Ellie had a friend here who was compassionate and empathic, I told myself. Indeed, Georgie seemed to share her friend's sorrow almost too much, but at least Ellie now had the support of someone she knew and trusted.

Georgie looked up at me from the floor. "Chloe?" She wiped her eyes. "How did you find out about this?"

I explained about the cooking demonstration that Digger was to have done for Hank, Kyle, and me, and I described arriving at his place to find the aftermath of the fire. "You knew Digger, too, obviously. I'm so sorry."

Georgie nodded. "Yes, I did. And my boyfriend, Jay, had actually been in a friendly rivalry with Digger for the job at the Penthouse. He's the sous-chef now, though. Ellie and I are going to be servers there." She glanced at Ellie, and the two fell apart. "I'll have to let him know, too."

Ellie had told me that the chef who'd come in second for the job was furious. Was that someone else? But now wasn't the time to straighten out the confusion, and I had no reason to care about who had or hadn't become the executive chef at the Penthouse. Georgie's boyfriend, Jay, would presumably take over for Digger. I didn't envy him having to jump in at the last minute to get the restaurant ready to open. As I knew from watching Josh prepare for Simmer's opening, he'd have a ton of work in front of him. Also, unless Digger had kept all of his plans at work, everything he'd slaved over must have been lost in the fire, so his successor would have to start from scratch. But maybe the new executive chef would have wanted to make the job all his own, anyway.

"I'm so sorry to have had to break the news," I said. "I should get going and leave you two alone." I rose from the couch and walked to the door.

"Thank you, Chloe," Ellie whispered. She reached for Georgie, who joined her on the couch.

I left the two tearful girls and drove toward home. The sky had clouded over and darkened the city. The gloomy atmosphere fit my mood. I shut off the radio, mainly to avoid hearing music that I would then forever associate with Digger's death. I'd had high hopes that the day would go well for Digger and for me. Instead, it had turned into a nightmare. Whenever things went wrong in my life, I wanted to fix them by taking constructive action, but there was no fixing this situation. I pulled into my parking spot in front of my condo and looked up at the familiar brown house. It felt good to be home. I shuffled up the back steps to the third floor and opened the door, where Inga the white fluffball of a cat stood meowing at me as if she knew how I felt and was waiting to take care of me. Stupid, I know, but I choose to believe it. I dropped my tote to the floor, threw my coat on the coffee table, and scooped up my girl, who purred melodically.

Still hugging the sympathetic little cat, I grabbed the phone and curled up on the couch. For some reason, I was seized by the urgent impulse to tell someone about Digger. Although he'd had friends and family who'd have to hear the news, it really wasn't my responsibility to inform them. Besides, in the tight-knit restaurant community, word would spread quickly. Someone, probably the police, would find and inform Digger's family. But what about Josh? I couldn't stand the thought of his hearing about Digger's death through the grapevine. He should hear from someone close to him. Of course, Josh's former sous-chef and former roommate, Snacker, could tell him, but as much as I loved Josh's crazy friend, he was not one to count on for a delicate, sensitive delivery. I called Adrianna.

"Hi, Chloe. What are you doing home already? Aren't you supposed to be feasting on delicious food at Digger's? Did you call to gloat?"

At the sound of Adrianna's voice, I started crying, and it took ages to compose myself enough to explain that Digger had died in a fire. When I could finally breathe normally, I described the morning in detail. "And I can't help worrying about Josh. Do you think I should get in touch with him?"

"This is just terrible," Ade said. "I'm in shock. What a horrible way to die! Oh, poor Digger. Well, do you have Josh's new phone number?"

"No. I think I still have his e-mail address, but that wouldn't be right. I can't send him an e-mail telling him that Digger is dead," I said with a sniffle. "And I don't want him to think that I'm using Digger's death as an excuse to contact him. But maybe that's what I want to do!" I wailed. Josh had been my rock for the past year; I was used to leaning on him. I still had Adrianna, but Josh had been a strong force in my life in a totally different way. I missed him more than ever. I missed him way too much for my own good.

"Chloe, I hate to say this, because I can tell how much you want to talk to Josh, but you know he'll hear about Digger from one of his friends. He knows tons of people in Boston, and he'll hear. You've been working so hard to get over him."

I blew my nose. "You're right. I'm moving on with my life. He moved on with his, right? He could have stayed in Boston instead of going to Hawaii without me, but he didn't. I'll just have to be sad about Digger without Josh," I announced as defiantly as I could.

"Listen, Chloe, I know you've had a crappy morning, but is there any chance you'd be up for doing me a favor?" I heard Patrick gurgling cutely in the background. "I hate to ask, but—"

"Anything," I said. "What do you need?"

"I was wondering if you could watch the baby for me this afternoon? Just for a few hours? I'm so desperate to get out of the house for a little bit, and a girl I used to work with said she could squeeze me in for a cut and color at four today. She just called me to say she had a cancellation, but I totally get it if you aren't up to it."

Not up to it? A few hours with the cutest cuddlebug in the world would cheer up and distract me. "I'd love to. Do you want to drop him off here? Around three thirty?" I turned a guilty eye to the hall closet, which was crammed full of outrageously expensive baby supplies. I'd paid for them with money that I still owed to the credit-card company, but I'd known that Patrick would spend time at my place and hadn't wanted Ade and Owen to haul stuff back and forth. This occasion was an excellent example of why I needed the baby supplies; having Patrick here would justify my purchases as necessary expenses.

"Are you sure you're up for it?" Adrianna asked. "Because I could try to get another appointment."

"No way. I want time with my buddy," I insisted. "See you then."

I took a scalding shower. Although the fire had been extinguished by the time I'd reached Digger's, the horrible odor that had enveloped his street seemed to cling to me. I washed my hair twice and doused myself in orange-and-honey-scented bath gel. Later, I spent a few hours trying to focus on my schoolwork, but images of burning buildings won out against rational thought, and I made almost no headway in my reading. I scanned the notes I had taken on the clients I saw at my internship and tried to think about other people's problems instead of my own.

Just as I was setting up Patrick's Pack 'n Play—a little portable crib and infant play area (not that I was expecting to let the gorgeous one out of my arms)—Kyle called.

"Chloe, I am so sorry about this morning. Not only for the fire that killed your friend, but also for my father's behavior. It's the way he is, but it was inexcusable. I just dropped him at the airport, so at least he's out of our hair for the time being."

My stomach churned when Kyle said *killed,* but I appreciated his apology. "Thanks so much. I'm still in shock," I said. "I can't really process what's happened yet."

"Of course. Listen, if you're up for it, I'd love to take you to dinner tonight. I have a seven o'clock reservation at Incline, in the Seaport district."

"That would be lovely," I said honestly. "I'll meet you there?"

"I'll come pick you up, if you like," Kyle offered. *Ohhh . . .* so maybe this was a date? "I have some more material to give you. The papers from the other night were only the tip of the iceberg. That is, if you're still interested in working on the cookbook?"

"Of course I'm still interested."

"Great. I don't want you to have to schlep all this stuff home with you, so this way I can drop it at your house. Six thirty sound okay?"

"Sure." I gave him my address and hung up, perfectly happy to have an excuse to cut my studying short. Patrick and Ade would be here soon, and I'd have to figure out what I was wearing to dinner with Kyle. Incline was a chic, intimate little restaurant that practically screamed romance— small tables, candles everywhere, soft background music, the whole shebang. When I'd gone there with my gay friend Doug, we'd nodded politely at our server's efforts to promote our supposed romance. The two of us hadn't really longed to be left alone, and we hadn't been eager to share a heart-shaped dessert. Luckily, I'd never eaten there with Josh, so I wouldn't be overwhelmed with memories of—*Damn!* I shut my eyes, refusing to tear up over my ex. Again, I briefly wondered about the possibility that Josh had been at Digger's last night, but I dismissed the idea. If Digger had known that Josh was going to be in town, he'd have said so when we'd talked on the phone.

I picked through my wardrobe and chose a short black skirt that I paired with a white shell and a cream-colored sheer cardigan. I'd put on tall black boots and look like a million bucks for Kyle. Josh could go to hell.

SEVEN

"NOW that is a gorgeous baby!" Kyle beamed at Patrick, who snuggled cozily in my arms, wrapped in a new fleece blanket that I'd unearthed from the closet of baby stuff.

"Isn't he the best?" I rubbed the peach fuzz on the baby's head and then kissed his nose. "I cannot get enough of him."

"Is, uh . . . is he yours?" Kyle stood in my living room holding an alarmingly large cardboard box that presumably held cookbook material. "You haven't said anything about being married or having a boyfriend or . . ."

"No, no." I smiled. "He's not mine. This is Patrick, Adrianna's baby. She went to get her hair done. She should be back any minute. I'm definitely not married and not dating anyone." I cringed. Could I be more obvious? But Kyle did look exceedingly handsome tonight. Again, he had on a suit, and although I didn't usually gravitate toward the stockbroker look, I was willing to expand my horizons. There was something sexy about his being all covered up in layers of clothing. I briefly wondered what was under that button-down. True, Kyle had a beast of a father—I couldn't imagine having that dreadful Hank Boucher as a father-in-law—but . . . Wait a minute! What the heck was I doing even considering Kyle as potential husband material? "I'm Patrick's godmother, so I get to spoil him to pieces. You can put that box down anywhere, Kyle."

"Thanks." Kyle couldn't keep his eyes off the baby. A good sign! The man loved children and probably wanted a family of his own.

"Here, why don't you hold Patrick for a minute, and I'll put the material on my desk." I rose from the couch and passed the baby to Kyle. "Just keep him close to your body. He likes being held tightly."

I helped position the baby in the crook of Kyle's arm. Cooing and sighing, the easygoing Patrick nestled right in. Reluctantly, I approached the box that my employer had set down. *Ugh.* I had just started to make progress on the first, much smaller, batch of notes Kyle had given me, and now I had this new mess to tackle. How on earth could Kyle imagine that randomly tossing papers into a big box was any way to approach writing? What if I handled my graduate school work like this? What if spent the semester haphazardly flinging notes into a box? Well, maybe Kyle was overzealous in his research and too busy to impose any coherent order on all of his findings. I carried the box to the bedroom and set it on a chair. Hours and hours of deciphering and typing lay ahead of me, but I would, of course, be paid for my time.

I heard the unofficial back door to the apartment open, the door at the top of the wooden fire escape that everyone in the building used as an outside staircase. Then I heard Adrianna's voice: "Oh, hi, Kyle."

When I stepped into the living room, Adrianna looked at me quizzically, as if she wanted to ask what Kyle was doing in my apartment holding her baby.

"Hi, Ade." I smiled at her. Her hair was now gloriously tinted in various shades of blonde that lit up her whole face, and her rose-colored tweed coat brought out the pink in her cheeks. After a few hours away from her baby, she looked as refreshed as if she'd had ten straight hours of sleep followed by a day at a spa. "Kyle and I are going to dinner at Incline," I told her. "Part of our cookbook research."

Adrianna's eyes widened. "That place is supposed to be fabulous." She reached for Patrick. "Kyle, you're a natural with kids. Patrick tends to fuss when people he doesn't know hold him, but he really seems taken with you."

"The feeling is mutual. He's absolutely adorable." Kyle beamed at the two. "I love kids. I hope to have my own someday."

Ade winked at me, none too subtly. "Well, I should get home. Owen should be back soon. He's grilling burgers again, if you can believe it. I'm probably going to start mooing any day now."

"Why don't you come to dinner with us? You can bring Patrick," Kyle offered.

"Thanks, but I'm beat. Patrick has taken to nocturnal living. He was up most of last night, which means I was up most of last night. Owen insists that he gets up every time Patrick does, but what he really means is that he is *disturbed* every time the baby cries. I'm the one who actually gets up and has to stay awake feeding him." She rolled her eyes, but she smiled as she tossed her blonde mane to the side. "Enjoy your meal. I expect a detailed report on how delicious everything is. Thanks so much, Chloe. I feel like a new woman after getting my hair done. And Kyle, it was really nice to see you again."

Kyle nodded at Ade. "You, too. You'll have to come out another night with us. We'll have more restaurants to try out. I'd love your input."

I hugged Ade and Patrick good-bye and promised to call her tomorrow with a rundown of tonight's food.

By the time we were seated at Incline, I was ravenous. Taking care of Patrick wasn't a hardship, but it did require a lot of energy and left little time to snack. The stress of the horrible morning had depleted me, too. I scooted my chair close to the table and checked out Kyle. He really was very good looking, especially in the light of the candle at our table. I loved his rough stubble and the golden streaks in his hair. Did Kyle think that I, too, looked good by candlelight? I'd changed into my carefully chosen outfit, spritzed on some perfume, and touched up my lipstick before we'd left. Even though this was a business dinner, we could still get swept away by the romantic atmosphere. The walls in the long, narrow restaurant had been painted chocolate brown, and the dark room was just as cozy as I remembered.

I tucked my hair behind my ears and leaned in a bit. "So your father has left Boston already? Where is he off to now?"

Kyle sighed and reached for his wine. "Yes, he's gone, thank God. I think he and his trophy wife are off to Telluride for most of the week. I don't think I could have taken much more of him. My father is riled up about this book, and he's really riding me to move it along. And I do want to make it happen. I think it could be a really successful start to the series."

As I stared at him—and tried not to salivate—I could see that behind the well-groomed façade was a very exhausted guy. During the short encounter I'd had with Hank Boucher, I found him draining, so I could only imagine what it was like to spend days rather than just minutes or hours with the domineering chef. "Okay, so what's your plan for putting the book together?"

"Oh . . ." Kyle shifted in his chair. "I'm not clear on that yet. But I do have some ideas. Do you want to hear them?"

I grinned. Kyle was disorganized, but he was eager and interested. I said, "Shoot."

"There are lots of cookbooks out already that feature the big-name restaurants and chefs. Certain restaurants in every major city are always showcased in magazine and newspaper articles. Over and over, they're the ones that get the attention. Sometimes deservedly so. Sometimes not, if you ask me. I'd like to do something different with this book. What about the fantastic but unheard-of restaurant on a small side street that serves the best braised lamb shank? Or the neighborhood Greek place where the owner's mother rolls out phyllo dough by hand every day? All the spectacular ethnic restaurants in this city that cook up some of the best food in Boston but never get the spotlight? There are some very talented chefs who work at places that never get the attention they should because they don't have the financial means to market themselves and to buy high-priced ads in *Boston Magazine.*"

I nodded eagerly. "That's brilliant, Kyle. Hidden treasures. We could spotlight unknown chefs and get recipes from restaurants that really deserve praise."

"As much as I love eating at restaurants like this one, the chef and the owner here don't need the publicity. And honestly? Half the time the food at these places is so overrated that it's obscene. Most of what's in that box I brought to your house are pieces I started on chefs at those unheard-of places. I'd like to focus on the small places that diners would love if they knew about them."

"Yes, but from a marketing standpoint, I think we should do a mix of high-end, well-known restaurants and the unknown ones that we really love. The big names will help sell the book." I began a mental list of my favorite hole-in-the-wall places to eat. "I haven't seen what's in the new box of material," I said. "I don't know where you've been already. But do you have any particular restaurants in mind? Have you been to Boston before or is this your first time?"

"Actually, I went to school here for a short time, so I know the city a bit."

Before I could ask where, a server arrived with our plates. One whiff of the bouillabaisse and I knew that I was in for a treat. I reached under the table and pulled out a notebook.

One of us had to take notes about our plans for the book, and the last thing I needed was to have to decipher yet more of Kyle's illegible scribbling. "Let's start by making a preliminary list of restaurants and types of restaurants. Tell me all of the places you've already eaten at, which chefs you've interviewed, and who has given you recipes. And what other restaurants are on your list to try."

I wrote furiously as Kyle did his best to recollect where he'd been and whom he'd interviewed. I was hoping that if he spelled out the information, I'd be able to make sense of the pile of notes that awaited me back home. As it was, I ended up having to remind Kyle of a number of restaurants that were mentioned in the notes I'd already typed up. I gripped my pen tightly as I patiently prompted him to wrack his brain and remember meals he'd had. "And where else would you like to try?"

"Jasper White's Summer Shack, Oleana, Mistral, L'espalier, Harvest—"

I produced an exaggerated snore. "Kyle!"

"What? What did I say?" He wasn't joking; he looked truly dumbfounded.

I dropped my pen in exasperation. "Those are arguably some of the best, most famous restaurants in Boston."

"Yes? So?"

"Exactly the kinds of places you just said you didn't want to focus on."

"Oh. I guess you're right. It's just that my father mentioned those and . . . well, it *is* his name on the book."

My guess was that Hank Boucher was as unimpressed with Kyle's progress on the book as I was and that he'd shouted out restaurant names in an attempt to prompt his son to do something—anything—about the book.

"Fine," I said. "We can use the famous restaurants, but once we visit the kinds of undiscovered places you were describing earlier, we'll add them in and have a good balance that will impress Mr. Boucher."

Kyle brightened. "There's a little Italian restaurant just outside of Kenmore Square that I've been dying to go to. How about we start with that one? Friday night?"

"Agreed. That's the kind of place that might be a hidden gem. Maybe we'll leave with an amazing family recipe for *bracciole*."

Kyle rubbed his hands together in excitement. "Yes, exactly." He looked directly at me, smiled, and then reached across the table and brushed his hand across mine. "What would I do without you?"

EIGHT

DURING the next week, I divided my time equally between school and Kyle's notes—or an effort to make sense
of them, anyway. My classes this semester were slightly
better than they'd been the previous year, mostly because
I had more electives this term than ever before. I'd chosen
my classes with an eye for ones that would irritate me as
little as possible. It amazed me that no one from my graduate school had shown up at my place to demand that I immediately remove myself from the program. Since I was far
from the model social-work student, I did my best not to
call attention to myself, lest the dean expel me for failure to
show even the slightest hint of enthusiasm for my impend-
ing profession.

I blamed my lack of militant devotion on my dead uncle Alan, who had inserted an infuriating clause into his will that made my inheritance contingent on the completion of a graduate program. *Any* graduate program. I could hear his desperation from the grave. I found it mildly insulting that my uncle had thought so little of my professional drive that he'd had to manipulate me into pursuing higher education. Having chosen social work on a whim, I'd regretted the choice almost every day since. My few bursts of interest had been short lived. I'd made few friends at school, undoubtedly because my fellow students smelled my loathing for social work. Also, I consistently failed to show up at the state house for various protests, and I avoided letter-writing "parties" where I was expected to devote hours to composing thoughtful or irate letters to senators and representatives. I refused to study in the library, which I entered only when necessary and which I fled as soon as possible. I could practically hear my classmates groan when I was assigned to one of their study groups, since I was unable to speak passionately about topics such as narrative therapy and ethics in medical settings.

My dissatisfaction increased when an Internet search revealed that instead of enduring the classes that I hated, I could have enrolled at what were probably nonexistent universities that offered interestingly titled online courses that would have required no interaction with anyone: "You Can't Make Me! Highly Effective Treatments for Resistant Clients" and "Can We Meet at Starbucks? Clients and Ethical Issues." I loved the idea of courses with dialogue in the titles, but my school offered no such inspiring classes. As I hated to admit, there were, however, elements of school that I enjoyed. Granted, most of my courses this semester had generic, meaningless names like "Working Across Boundaries" and "Using Theories in Social Work." Consisting as it did of vague concepts, the content of the courses made it easy to write essays. But I did enjoy some of my studies. My class on attachment had been quite interesting, and the class on working with individuals was coming in handy at my internship at the mental health center, so there were moments when I didn't cuss out my program. Not many moments! But a few. Still, my strategy was to keep my head down and barrel ahead as I awaited the arrival of my May graduation. As much as I disliked school, I also couldn't accept doing poorly, so I busted my hump to get good grades.

As for my job, I stayed up late every night that week working on Kyle's box of chicken-scratch writing. Touched by his desperate desire to present the evidence of capable work to his famous father, I dutifully transcribed all of his notes and recipes, and I spent an excessive amount of time converting scrawled bits of chef interviews into coherent paragraphs. The file on my computer was growing, but it was nowhere near close to being book length. At the end of every day, I e-mailed Kyle the number of hours I had worked. On Friday afternoon, when I received an overnighted envelope with a check made out to me from Hank Boucher's office, I blinked and read the amount again. I hadn't added up my hours in my head, but the number was much bigger than I'd expected.

At seven o'clock on that same Friday night, I took the T and went to meet Kyle at the Italian restaurant he'd chosen,

Contadino's. It was so cold out that I was glad I'd worn my puffy down parka, but why I'd bought a white parka was beyond me. I should've known that it would have a one-in-six-million chance of staying white for long. But the cute fake-fur collar had suckered me in. Standing outside the restaurant, I crossed my arms to stay warm and stared in the window at a neon sign that beckoned me to come in and try the AL YOU CAN EAT P ST . So the sign was missing a few letters. That was okay. And the dirty windows could be cleaned. Despite the frumpy exterior, the place deserved a shot; it was exactly the kind of hole-in-the-wall that might serve up fantastic fare. The door squeaked loudly as I entered what honesty forces me to call the ratty restaurant. I cringed at the worn carpet and red pleather booths. Plastic leather would've been bad enough. But pleather with rips? I joined Kyle, who was already seated at one of the booths. Except for Kyle and one table of rowdy, drunk college kids, the place was empty.

Kyle stood to greet me. I had dressed casually tonight, but Kyle was wearing one of his requisite suits, this one dark brown with a red patterned tie.

"Hi, Kyle," I said as I slid into the booth. "Have you been waiting long?"

"Nope, I just got here myself," he said.

A waitress walked by and tossed menus onto the table without pausing to see whether we wanted drinks. I eyed her suspiciously and picked up one of the laminated menus. It took only a quick skim to see that the dishes were typical of many old-school Italian restaurants: lots of pasta with a few sauce and meat options, *piccata* this,

Parmesan that. Still, I resolved not to judge the food until it was served. After all, this unpromising dump could be the source of the most flavorful red sauce in Boston. I did, however, decide not to risk ordering seafood. The odds felt good that the kitchen was hideously unsanitary, and I didn't happen to have a craving for rotten mussels. Our disgruntled waitress eventually stooped to taking our order, but she managed to act positively put out by our presence and annoyed at us for wanting something to eat—in a restaurant, of all places.

"So how is your friend Adrianna doing?" Kyle asked as he moved to take a drink from his water glass. "Have you two been friends for a long time?"

"Don't drink that," I said, touching his wrist. "The glass is dirty."

Kyle peered at his water and frowned. "Indeed it is." A large glob of some dark substance clung to the inside of the glass. He set it down and pushed it to the center of the table.

"Adrianna is doing well. I've hardly seen her this week, though, since I've been so busy with school and the cookbook work. But we've known each other since high school, so we each understand when the other gets bogged down with life. The poor girl has been so tired, of course, because of Patrick. I don't think she was prepared for how stressful being a parent is."

Kyle nodded. "Well, she doesn't show it. Does her husband, Owen, help out much?"

"Sure. It's a rough time for him with work, though. He gets up at about four thirty in the morning to get the seafood orders for his restaurants, and then he isn't home again until five or so. Sometimes later if people call because they ran out of tuna or forgot to order scallops or something. And his income is dependent on the market, of course. He determines the price for what he sells, and there's only so much he can raise the cost of fish. Sometimes he makes only pennies per pound on some items. Oh, and he pays for his gas, too. It's a rough business, but some weeks are better than others. And his schedule is really good. He's at home with Ade and Patrick every night."

"He must be exhausted, though, when he comes home."

"True, but at least he has a regular job now. This is much better than the puppeteer phase."

Kyle laughed. I admired the small dimples that appeared on his cheeks. "Well," he said, "Patrick is adorable. He must be good company for Adrianna, huh?"

"That bundle of baby yumminess is more amazing than I could have imagined. I knew that I'd be loopy about my best friend's baby, but I had no idea how deeply attached I'd become. And so quickly. He's only three months old, but I can't imagine not having him in the world." I thought about my class on attachment and about how important and meaningful our familial, romantic, and friendship attachments were. I knew how strong my attachment to Patrick was, how innate it felt and how uncomplicated it was. Since Patrick was Adrianna's son, she must have magnified versions of those same feelings. "I know he's only a baby, and I'm not his mother, but I can't help feeling that he and I have a truly special bond. There's just something magical that takes over when I'm with him."

Kyle nodded and looked at me with kindness in his eyes. "I could see that when I came to your house the other day. He's very lucky to have you in his life, Chloe."

When the waitress brought our food, I managed to refrain from wrinkling my nose at the glob of thick spaghetti slathered with lumpy Alfredo sauce. Kyle looked equally horrified by his chicken Marsala. A few small bites of our food confirmed that some of the time, looks are not deceiving.

Kyle rested his fork on his plate and shut his eyes, laughing softly. "Okay, this restaurant has officially been cut from the list of possibilities for the cookbook."

"You think?" I asked with a grin.

"Let's get out of here." Kyle didn't bother getting a check for our pathetic meal. He stood up and threw some cash on the table. "This meal isn't worth deducting as a business expense," he joked.

Kyle held the door open for me as we exited into the busy scene in Kenmore Square. The college kids were out in full force, and groups of laughing students brushed past us on their way to the bars. Kyle offered to walk me to my car, but I'd taken the T. Public transportation was easy for me because the C Line ran right into Cleveland Circle, which was only a few blocks from my place.

"I'm not letting you ride home with all these drunken idiots," Kyle said as he waved his arm around us. "A pretty girl like you would be fending off ogling frat boys the whole way home. Come on. I'll give you a ride." He flashed me a sexy smile and held his arm out for me. "Madame? Or should I say, *signora?*"

"Ugh," I groaned. "No Italian right now, please!" I looped my arm through his and let him escort me to his car.

I stared at Kyle as he drove us down Beacon Street toward Boston College and listened to him ramble about other restaurants we could try. He really was good looking and genuine and . . . well, normal. Plus, he drove a badass Audi with leather seats and a kickin' sound system. I let my focus drift over his body and admired his solid chest and narrow waist. When I worked my gaze back up to his arms, I wondered what sort of defined muscles might be lurking under that suit of his. His lips were full and sort of . . .

"Chloe?"

"Yes?" I whispered a bit too breathlessly.

"This is your turn, right?"

"My turn?"

"To your house." Kyle pointed to a street sign.

"Oh. Yes, that's it." As we drove up the side street, I fidgeted nervously and flipped my hair over my shoulder twice.

Kyle pulled up to the curb and set the car in park. "Sorry dinner didn't go as planned, but I'll make it up to you. You pick the next restaurant, okay?" He touched his hand to my arm and smiled.

I held his look. We were having a moment! I could feel it! "I had a great time," I said in a voice that I hoped was steamy and seductive. "I really did." With no forethought, I leaned awkwardly across the gearshift and flung my arms around Kyle's neck. I touched the back of his head with my fingers as I pressed myself against him. I inhaled. He smelled like the icky Italian restaurant, but I couldn't fault him for that, especially because I must've smelled the same way. I was making my first move since Josh. And it felt wonderful! I was moving on, charming new men, and leading an exciting single life! I buried my head in his neck and then kissed him softly there, letting my tongue tease him. Kyle patted my back, slowly at first, and then suddenly with great urgency. Well, I thought, this is an odd way to show affection, but rapid back-patting was apparently Kyle's way of encouraging me, of letting me know that he was responding to my sexy neck-kissing move.

"Oh! Plowee!" Kyle's voice sounded weirdly muffled and frantic.

I yanked myself away. My winter jacket had puffed up around my shoulders and was pressing against his face. I was suffocating the man!

"Sorry! Sorry about that!" I stammered as I fumbled with my seatbelt. "So, so sorry!" I yanked repeatedly on the door handle, willing the stupid thing to open and free me from further embarrassment. "What's wrong with the door? It won't open!" I pounded my shoulder against it just as Kyle hit the unlock button, and as the door flew open, I lurched violently to the right. Amazingly, I caught myself, dangled precariously over the curb, and held still, possibly in hope of finding a graceful way to make a recovery. But there was none. I waved my left hand in Kyle's direction, and he grabbed hold and pulled me upright. I did my best to compose myself and appear relaxed. "Well, thank you for dinner. I'll call you in the next few days with an update on the cookbook progress. Good night." I beamed idiotically and stepped out of the car.

"Chloe, it's okay," Kyle called after me. He rolled down his window and continued talking. "You don't have to be embarrassed. Please, come back."

I waved as I crossed the street. "Of course not. Everything is fine!" I said with a chipper ring in my voice. "Talk to you soon!" I tried to stroll casually to the front door, but my body wouldn't listen, and I practically ran up the walkway. *What the hell is wrong with me?* I unlocked the front door and stomped angrily up the stairs to the third floor. *I am a sex-starved lunatic who just molested and nearly asphyxiated my boss.* I opened the door to my condo, yanked off my stupid puffy coat, and hurled it across the living room, startling Inga and Gato, who went running for the bedroom. "Sorry," I muttered. "I'm having an off night, okay, kitties?"

I stormed into the kitchen. It took more than humiliation to kill my appetite; I was hungry. I pushed food around in the fridge and assessed what I had to work with. *Aha, perfect.* I pulled out a hydroponic tomato that I'd paid a fortune for, some heavy cream, an egg, and grated Parmesan cheese. I turned on the oven and then sliced the top off the tomato, scooped out the pulp, and flipped the tomato upside down onto a paper towel. I sat in a chair and stared at the tomato while it drained.

I was totally annoyed with myself. What had possessed me to fling myself at Kyle like that? Furthermore, what was up with that weird neck thing I'd done? Who does that? Obviously I'd been reading too many of those vampire romance books. Stupid Stephenie Meyer. Well, reading about vampires was going to stop immediately. Who knew what more I was capable of? One more vampire read, and I might actually have bitten Kyle. I dropped my head into my hands and shook my stupid skull back and forth. *I'll just pretend this never happened*, I thought. The next time I see Kyle, I'll behave like a completely normal, nonfreakish employee.

I turned the tomato upright and set it into a small baking dish. I broke the egg into the tomato, poured in a spoonful of cream, and then topped the cream with some of the grated Parmesan. In twenty minutes the egg would be set and I'd have a hot, comforting meal to soothe my frazzled nerves. And the tub of Friendly's Forbidden Chocolate in the freezer wouldn't hurt, either. Ah, food.

NINE

AFTER attacking Kyle Boucher, the least I could do was devote my Saturday to his cookbook. Gastronomic repentance, I suppose. My success in pulling the book together would prove that I was not some basket case, but a skilled assistant. Besides, the hefty paycheck I'd just received was no small motivator. Even if my bizarre display of affection had spoiled any chance of a relationship with Kyle, I could still whip through the cookbook and rake in some money.

Easier said than done. I frowned at the computer screen as I scrolled down my rough and incomplete draft of the table of contents. The worst problem was the existence of substantial gaps in some categories and an overabundance of material in others. Twenty-six soups and only four desserts?

And five different recipes for roast chicken. Five? I like a good roast chicken as much as the next person, but the recipes were nearly identical. I made a note to delete four and to keep my favorite, the simple salt-crusted chicken that was bound to taste fantastic, judging from the aroma emanating from my kitchen. It had taken me all of six minutes to rub the chicken with olive oil, salt, and pepper, stuff it with rosemary and basil, and then cover it with coarse salt. When it was done, I'd break off the salt crust and dive in. The need to test the recipes provided a good excuse to try out some of the more delicious-sounding ones. Plus, the chef who'd been the source of this recipe had actually taken the time to write a coherent list of ingredients and clear directions. Most chefs were impossible. One recipe I'd tackled earlier this morning was for an Asian-style hotpot that would serve sixty people. Sixty! I'd never heard of half of the ingredients, and the instructions were confusing. Chefs just didn't seem to understand that the rest of us lacked their inherent brilliance in the kitchen; we needed to be told what to buy and what to do.

Kyle and I would have to get new recipes for the short-changed categories in the cookbook, and we'd have to avoid getting yet more duplicate and triplicate recipes, but I hated to sound picky and bossy in asking chefs for the favor of sharing recipes. *We need a beef dish that does not have potatoes or leeks but does have cumin and rutabagas. And no roast chicken!* What I needed to do was to browse through a great chef's recipes and pull out what we needed.

Digger, I thought with a smile. Digger had had recipes. If I could find them, if they hadn't burned with the build-

ing, we could include them in the book as a wonderful trib-
ute to him. Plus, Digger cooked damn well. No one would
imagine that including him in the book was an act of pity.
Ellie would probably like the idea as much as I did. I even
had the feeling that, in spite of her grief, she'd be pleased to
have Digger gain the posthumous celebrity.

I called Ellie and had to let the phone ring repeatedly
before she picked up. "Hello." Her voice was weak and
hoarse.

"Ellie, it's Chloe. How are you holding up?" I asked.

"I'm not doing very well," she said as she burst into tears.
"I had to identify Digger's body."

"I'm so sorry." I let her cry for a few moments before
presenting my idea. "I think Digger would like the idea of
being published, don't you?"

"Yes, I do," she sniffed. "I think that's really lovely."

"Do you know where he kept his recipes? Are they at the
restaurant, or do you have any?"

"No." She managed a small laugh. "He would never have
kept them where someone else could have access to them.
You know chefs. They guard their private recipes with their
lives." She paused. What a choice of words. "Oh God!" Ellie
started crying again, and I had to wipe my own eyes. I heard
her take a deep breath. "I had to identify his body, Chloe.
It was awful." I waited while she sobbed. "Anyhow, no, I
don't have any of his recipes, unfortunately. Digger didn't
need me to help him cook. He kept them in a messenger
bag in his apartment. It was usually in the bedroom by the
front door, which isn't that close to the kitchen, so maybe it
wasn't destroyed. That's the room he used as his office. I'll

go over there later today or tomorrow and let you know if I can find the bag. This is a really nice idea. Thanks for thinking of including him."

"Are you sure you're up to going over there? Do you want me to help you? Or maybe your friend Georgie can go with you?" I suggested.

"No. I need to do it. I've been putting it off, but I need to see what I might be able to keep of his. You know, as a reminder or whatever. Besides, I've got some of my stuff there, too. Or I had some. I'll call you tomorrow."

I hung up and went to check on the salt-crusted chicken. I opened the oven, pulled out the roasting pan, took a good whiff, and smiled. The potatoes I'd baked were also done, so I tossed together a salad and enjoyed a fabulous early dinner. It was only five o'clock. Living alone was not heinously depressing, I told myself; it had its advantages. For instance, I could eat whenever I wanted. When I'd finished my meal, I popped Season Four of *The Closer* into the DVD player and lay down on the couch. Another wild night at Chez Chloe, right? At least I was getting a lot of sleep these days. With Josh in my life, I'd hardly slept, or so it now seemed. I used to wait up at night to see him when he got off work, and then we'd be up late doing wonderfully wicked things to each other, but I'd still have to get up for classes in the morning. Not that I'd cared about being tired, but why not appreciate a good night's sleep now?

When the phone awakened me the next morning, I rolled over in bed and glanced at the clock. It was ten. I'd slept for twelve hours, maybe a bit too long. I lifted the phone to my ear and curled back up under the covers.

"Chloe? It's Ellie. Digger is a stupid son of a bitch!" Her voice was loud and forceful; she sounded nothing like the soft-spoken, crying girl I'd talked to yesterday.

I yanked the covers off my head and sat bolt upright. "What's going on?"

"After everything I did for him? He can go to hell! In fact, that's probably where he is right now, and he can burn there for all of eternity!"

"Did something happen, Ellie?"

"Yes, something happened. What happened is that Digger is a goddamn asshole, and so screw him! At least I'm not crying anymore, so that's a good thing, right?"

"If you think so," I said doubtfully. "I'm not really sure what's going on. Did you go to his apartment?"

"The building is condemned, so I couldn't get in. Not that I give a crap anyway! I don't want to see anything that reminds me of him, anyway, so don't ask me to go back there! I hate him!" she screamed into the phone.

"What am I missing here, Ellie?"

"Digger is a self-centered, smug jackass! That's what you're missing." Ellie abruptly hung up.

I flopped back on the bed. What the heck was that all about? One minute Digger's girlfriend was a crying mess, and now she's a swearing mess. And so much for the recipes. I couldn't very well call Ellie back now and insist that she sneak into a condemned building and search through the charred possessions of a dead man she suddenly hated.

But, I realized, there was nothing to stop me.

There'd be no one guarding the building. The police certainly had better things to do than assign officers to stand outside a burned-out building to prevent the illegal entry of cookbook assistants. At least I hoped they did. I didn't relish the prospect of going alone, but I couldn't think of anyone to enlist as an accomplice. Adrianna was far too glamorous to go galumphing around in an incinerated building, and since she was a mother, I couldn't ask her to do anything even slightly risky. Besides, if I told her about my plan, she'd try to prevent me from going. In contrast, Owen would be game, but now that he was a father, he was finally acting responsibly, and I shouldn't encourage bad behavior. My friend Doug was fastidious beyond words and wouldn't even consider accompanying me; the thought of even a hint of soot on his shoes would send him into convulsions. My sister, Heather, would never agree. Kyle was out of the question. At least for now.

So I was going to have to go alone. Fine. Another step marking my independence! I hopped up, started a pot of coffee, and tried to decide when to go. Daylight seemed none too smart, since the neighbors would be bound to notice me. Drawing on my in-depth study of adventurous undertakings—via TV and movies—I thought of *24* and asked myself, *What would Jack Bauer do?* Well, Jack had only twenty-four hours to do a lot more than look for recipes in an apartment, so unless I had to fit my plan in between disarming a nuclear bomb and torturing criminals, I didn't have Jack's time constraints. Good! If I went to Digger's when it was totally dark, I'd have to use a flashlight; the electricity must have been turned off. But a flashlight would attract attention and make me look like a burglar. Although I wasn't totally committed to social work, I wasn't about to abandon my career choice for life as a burglar, especially one who got caught. The best time seemed to be late afternoon, when it would be somewhat dark but when there would still be enough light coming through the windows for me to see my way around. And on my key chain was a penlight I could use if need be.

For the rest of the day, I puttered around the house nervously, waiting for the sky to start darkening, and when it did, I drove to Digger's. Dressing for my first breaking and entering had been a challenge. Nothing dressy, obviously, but I couldn't look suspicious, in case someone saw me and called the police. All black had seemed too obvious, so I'd gone with dark jeans, a dark ribbed turtleneck, and brown boots. I also did my hair and makeup. It might sound stupid to get dressed up to sneak into a condemned building, but I wanted to look normal and ordinary, as if I had some legitimate reason to be in the neighborhood and in Digger's apartment. I mean, rescuing recipes *was* legitimate, but it might not seem that way to spying neighbors. Or to the cops, either.

I parked a few buildings down from Digger's, locked the car, and pulled on a white fleece hat. I wanted to cover my red hair, which stood out and made me identifiable. Stupid hair! I walked assuredly toward the apartment and up a long driveway to the back of the building. Bold signs on the front door declared the building to be condemned, and plywood had been nailed over some of the lower windows. I tried to march with confidence and radiate an air of authority, as though I worked for the city or for some company that required me to inspect the premises. Aha! I could pretend to represent a homeowner's insurance company. From my purse, I retrieved a pen and one of the small notebooks I'd taken with me when I'd met Kyle. I furrowed my brow and stared intently at the building while I wrote in the notebook: *Very burned. Fire, obviously. Still stinky here.* There, that should fool anyone who might be watching me. If I had planned this masquerade ahead of time, I'd have brought a camera so that witnesses would see me taking pictures.

I rounded the back corner of the building and ascended the short flight of fire-escape stairs to Digger's back door. A hell of a lot of good the fire escape had done him! Ellie had given me no opportunity to ask to use her key; I prayed that I'd be able to get in. One look at the door told me that there'd be no need for a key. The door had obviously been smashed in, probably by the fire department. Splintered wood hung in jagged fragments behind yellow caution tape. I glanced left and right, and then ducked under the tape and into the kitchen.

The kitchen was a disaster. I felt sick as I looked at the remains of the cabinets. The little that was left of them was black and unsalvageable. The counters and floors were covered in ash and chunks of ceiling. The stench nearly made me gag. I didn't know whether its source was rotting food in the fridge or whether I was just smelling the fire; either way, the reek was nauseating. I suddenly wanted to move quickly. For the first time, it occurred to me that this place might have been condemned not simply as a matter of routine but for real safety reasons. I had no interest in having a support beam come crashing down on my head. Also, I'd miscalculated my time of arrival. It was darker inside than I would have liked; I should have arrived fifteen minutes earlier. Still, I could see that the kitchen opened onto a hallway, one that presumably would lead me to the bedroom, by the front door, that Digger had used as an office.

I gingerly stepped across and around the debris on the floor while holding out my arms to keep my balance. I kept my eyes focused exclusively on the area directly ahead of me; I wanted to see no more than was required to let me move safely. As much as possible, I avoided taking in the details of the scene, because every bit of damage made me acutely aware that the same fire that had caused the destruction surrounding me was the fire that had killed Digger. With each passing second, I longed more and more to escape the ruined apartment and the thoughts that it triggered. When I reached the hallway, my stomach dropped. Ahead of me was blackness. I took my key chain from my pocket and turned on the penlight. Its inadequate beam was only slightly better than no light at all, but the penlight did let me see a piece of supporting timber that hung from the ceiling and stretched down to reach the floor. Coming here at all felt like a colossally stupid idea.

Whimpering, I pressed myself against the filthy wall and slid past the fallen timber. Although I hated being here, I remained as determined as I'd been before to get the recipes and to memorialize Digger in a way he would like, and I realized that if I panicked and ran away, I'd end up having to return. Flashing the light in front of me, I saw that the windows over the front door were boarded up. To the right, a wide arch apparently opened to the living room. I passed one small doorway to what must have been Digger's bedroom, the place I was most reluctant to enter. I fervently hoped that his messenger bag would be in the front bedroom, his office, where Ellie had told me it was. Reaching the end of the hallway, I looked through an open door to the left, and tentatively shone my light around. From what I could see, there was significantly less fire damage here at the front of the apartment than there was toward the back. Still, there was plenty of plaster dust and soot.

Perhaps because the room was at the front of the building, by the street, all the windows had been boarded up, so I had only my penlight to guide me. I cautiously stepped in and made out a couple of bookshelves to my left. Across the room was a small desk that seemed like a likely place for Digger to have left his messenger bag. After checking for a clear path, I made my way to the desk, reached out to put my hand on the back of a chair, and looked quickly around for the bag. The top of the desk was covered in soot, but I could make out a very clear rectangular spot that was remarkably clean and, as I immediately realized, just about the size of a notebook computer. To the right of the desk, a printer sat on top of a stack of cinder blocks. I backed up and moved slowly to my left, but tripped over something large and lumpy on the floor and went crashing down.

I released a muffled shriek. *Please don't let it be a dead body, please don't let it be a dead body!* I repeated the plea over and over, as if it were a mantra. I could feel my arms shake, but I pushed myself up off the lump and realized that I'd tripped over a mattress. Digger had apparently used this room as a second bedroom and not just an office. I sighed, stood up, and smacked my back into something hard. A loud crash nearly sent me into cardiac arrest, but I whipped the light in the direction of the noise. I'd knocked over two milk crates filled with cookbooks. Okay, enough was enough! I was getting the messenger bag and getting the hell out of here. I planted my feet firmly on the floor and played the small light slowly and deliberately over every inch of the room.

There it was. That had to be it. An overstuffed messenger bag sat right by the doorway. Damn. If I'd looked carefully before entering the room, I could have avoided scaring myself to pieces. I got the bag, put the strap over my shoulder, and stepped into the hallway. Since I was right by the front door, I hoped to use it to make a quick escape that would spare me from backtracking down the hallway and through the kitchen. I located the front door, but just as I set my hand on the doorknob, a noise coming from the kitchen made me freeze.

I don't believe in ghosts, but I do believe in rats, and if I had to choose between running into one or the other, I'd pick ghosts. I furiously jiggled the doorknob, barely seeing what I was doing because my nerves were making the penlight shake and dance all over the place. Although the knob turned, the door didn't budge. *Dammit! It must be sealed.* It made no sense to have sealed the front door and not the back, but now was not the time to phone the city to complain about how its employees handled condemned buildings. The noise from the kitchen grew louder. Then it moved closer to me. I had a sudden, ardent wish that I'd been right about the rats. The sound of footsteps, however, told me that there was another person in the apartment.

I tried to talk myself out of my panic. There was no reason to imagine that this newcomer was a threat, I told myself. A neighbor who'd seen or heard me must have come to investigate. I struggled to make speedy plans. In this situation, what would an insurance company investigator say? I shifted the weight of Digger's bag on my shoulder and pivoted as smoothly as I could to face whoever was coming my way. Squinting into the bright beam of a flashlight, I was blinder than I'd been in complete darkness.

The light moved away from eyes, and I could see a man's figure approaching, a man who moved down the hallway much less clumsily than I had.

My trembling became uncontrollable. The man stepped close to me. His flashlight dropped to the floor as he moved in until he was only inches from me. Then he pressed his body against mine, pushing my back to the door, pinning me to it, keeping my knees from giving out on me.

"Chloe," he whispered, barely audible.

I could see nothing at all, but I could feel his hands on my waist, pulling me against him and then moving up my sides, across my back. His mouth found mine, and I could taste him as he started kissing me deeply. I stopped thinking and just let myself get lost in his taste and his feel. I lifted my hands to his face, touching his cheeks and then running my fingers through his hair. I wrapped my arms around his neck and held on tightly, barely able to breathe as he continued to kiss me relentlessly. Finally I pulled away enough to take in some air.

"Josh," I said. "Josh."

TEN

"JOSH," I repeated in disbelief. I moved my lips to his again, totally delirious and responding instinctively.

He nuzzled his cheek against mine. Feeling his warm breath on my ear, I shuddered.

"God, I missed you," he said, and I felt him move in to kiss me again.

Suddenly coming to my senses, I shoved him away with both hands. "What the hell are you doing here? You scared the crap out of me!"

"You don't feel scared to me." I could tell he was smiling. "What's with all the pushing?"

"I can push you if I feel like it!" I spun around and again yanked on the front door. I'd break it down if I had to. I felt

Josh reach up and heard him slide a dead bolt open. The door unexpectedly flew open, and I went sailing out into the cold air and ended up flailing around idiotically, tangled in a mess of yellow police ribbon.

"Chloe, stop moving," Josh instructed as he tried to free me from the caution tape.

Considering how pissed I suddenly was, he should have left me tangled up and heeded the neon yellow warning.

"Don't touch me!" I hollered as I barreled down the front steps. "How dare you try to untangle me after the horrific way you left!" I glared at him, finally getting a good look at the chef who had broken my heart only months before. Streetlights lit his face. It killed me to see that he looked even more gorgeous than ever. Lightened by the sun, his hair was blonder than before, and his skin was tan from those months in Hawaii. Damn, he looked hot! I was angrier than ever. "Do you have any idea what it's been like for me since you left? Do you? I'm so sick of crying that I can't cry anymore. You left me, Josh. With barely any explanation except to say that you got a great job offer in Hawaii. The next thing I knew, you were gone!"

Josh stood silently by the door as he absorbed my tirade. I found it satisfying that he looked crushed. Good! He deserved to feel hurt.

"I thought you loved me!" I screamed. Hot tears fell down my cheeks, and I didn't bother to wipe them away. "I thought you loved me," I repeated, my voice cracking.

Josh took a step forward, "Chloe, of course—"

"Stay away from me!" I ordered.

I heard a loud creak a few yards away and saw first a fist

and then a head sticking out a first-floor window in the building next to us. A man's voice demanded, "What the hell is going on out here now?"

I squinted in the dark. "Norris?" I could just make out the crabby neighbor I'd spoken with on the morning of the fire, the one who'd complained so much about Digger's cooking. "Hi, Norris. It's me, Chloe. From the other day."

"That building is condemned, young lady. Can't you read? I ought to call the police."

"Sorry to bother you. We're just . . ." I scowled at Josh and corrected myself. "I'm just leaving."

"Hey!" Norris snarled. "What's that?" he said, pointing to Digger's messenger bag. "Are you stealing now? Looting? Jesus Christ, that damned chef is causing as much trouble now that he's dead as he did when he was alive. All I want is peace and quiet. No noise, no smells, no women, and no robbers! Get outta here!" Norris pulled his head back into his apartment and slammed the window shut.

I started to walk quickly to my car but could hear Josh clamber down the front steps and follow me. I kept walking.

"Chloe? Chloe? Come on. Please talk to me," he said as he caught up to me. "Slow down, would you?"

"You want to talk? Talk to yourself all you want. I'm going home."

"Digger," he said. "At least talk to me about Digger."

I stopped but kept my back to Josh. Okay, I could do that. "How did you hear?" I asked sadly.

"Snacker called me. That's why I'm here."

"Yes, I figured it didn't have anything to do with me." I

gripped Digger's bag more tightly. "So what were you doing in his apartment?"

"This story about Digger causing the fire just isn't credible. Digger was a pro, Chloe. He was careful, and he'd never just leave something on the stove and forget it."

I faced Josh. "Is that what they're saying? All I heard is that the fire was an accident."

Josh nodded. "Yeah. It doesn't make any sense." He dropped his head. "Why didn't you call me and tell me about Digger?"

I shrugged. "It wasn't my place to anymore. I knew someone would get in touch with you, and obviously someone did. It didn't have to be me."

"It would've been nice if it'd been you."

"Yeah, Josh? A lot of things would've been nice," I spat back.

He bit his lip and stared at me. "So what were you doing here? What's in the bag?"

I continued walking. "I came to get Digger's recipes." I briefly explained about helping with Hank Boucher's cookbook and saw Josh's eyes widen at the mention of the celebrity chef's name. "I thought it would be good to include some of Digger's work, and his girlfriend, Ellie, seemed to agree. Well, at least she did at first. . . . Anyhow, I need to get home and start sorting through this stuff. Kyle will be expecting to hear from me." When we reached my car, I got in without glancing at Josh. Then I rolled down the window.

"Who's Kyle?" he asked.

"Kyle is . . . It doesn't matter. Do you, uh, do you need a ride?"

"No." Josh shook his head. "I have Snacker's car."

"Good. Tell Snacker I said hello."

"I'm staying with him in my old room until I find out what's going on here. The couple I work for was really understanding. They told me to take as much time as I needed."

"How nice for you," I said sharply.

"I'm not going back to Hawaii until I find out how Digger died. I think he was murdered, Chloe."

I gripped the steering wheel. I had no idea what to say. Something was off about Digger's death, but I wasn't jumping to the conclusion that he'd been deliberately killed. There was no reason to think so. Or was there?

"Listen, can we talk sometime?" he asked.

I started the engine. "I have to go, Josh." I rolled up the window.

"Chloe, come on!" He had the audacity to sound annoyed.

I took off, leaving Josh standing alone on the curb.

I flew down the street, my heart pounding and my brain full of four-letter words. I was positively bullshit about the run-in with Josh. I'd been completely unprepared. With no defenses at the ready, I'd fallen victim to my visceral reaction to Josh and had totally made out with him in the heat of the moment. If I'd been braced for an encounter with him and had been thinking rationally, none of that hot-and-heavy action would have occurred. At least, I didn't think so. It was some comfort that I'd yelled at him. If I'd been the reason he'd come back, maybe I'd have felt differently. I wasn't sure. But I couldn't fault him for the reason he'd returned. His close friend had just died, and he wanted to know how and why. Still, it had been easier to have Josh in Hawaii than it was to have him in Boston, that was for sure.

I vacillated between anger, desire, and depression as I drove home. My brain and my heart felt ready to explode. Even when I had reached the safety of my apartment, I was still agitated. I rushed through the living room and into the bedroom, where I simultaneously turned on my laptop and lifted the phone from the cradle to scan caller ID. No new calls. At the computer, I unblocked Josh's e-mail address from my message program and hit Send/Receive four times in a row. No new messages. Good, right? I didn't want Josh calling or e-mailing me, I told myself. That was why I'd changed my cell number and blocked his e-mail address in the first place. Of course, I'd kept my old landline number. There was that. Still, he was now in Boston, and how was I supposed to move on with him right here? I could practically feel his presence in the city, and my awareness that he was right nearby was going to make it almost impossible to block him out of my consciousness. Here I was, right now, poised by the phone and computer, waiting for some kind of contact from him! And if Josh did call or e-mail me, it would probably be to ask about Digger. On that topic, why was Josh so sure that Digger had been murdered? God, it was tragic enough that Digger had died in the fire. But murdered? I shook my head. Maybe Josh's suspicion was his way of trying to deal with the loss of his friend.

No matter where Josh was or what was going on with him right now, I had to focus on the rest of my life. School, for instance, still required a lot of work, and I had plenty of cookbook activities to distract me. Plus, the money was pretty damn good. I decided to take a quick look through Digger's bag in search of material for Hank Boucher's book.

I opened the messenger bag and cringed. The fabric of the messenger bag reeked of smoke, and the contents smelled equally foul. They consisted of exactly what I expected from a chef: large notebooks filled with scribbled recipes, a few typed pages with notes scrawled on them, and two small notebooks with more recipes, as well as permanent markers, a kitchen thermometer, and some inventory pages. God, he was worse than Kyle! This kind of chaos must be a man thing. But as I'd hoped, the disorganized bag was filled with mouthwatering menus and recipes. Everything about the contents of the bag was so Digger that I teared up as I deciphered his writing. What's more, I knew that Kyle would be as eager as I was to put some of Digger's recipes in the cookbook. There was a stromboli recipe that looked delicious. Digger had written, *Family recipe, good comfort food. Restaurant possibility or no?* Digger hadn't been sure that the stromboli would fit in at the Penthouse, but he'd clearly liked the homemade dough stuffed with fresh mozzarella and herbs. I'd have to copy this and make it myself. I could practically smell the dough baking just thinking about it!

I was feeling good about honoring Digger's memory when I came upon some of Josh's recipes in Josh's own handwriting. Running my hands over the familiar script, I felt terribly sad. The consolation I'd found in the thought of including Digger in the book suddenly vanished, and everything about the smoky bag felt heartbreaking, as if there were nothing left of Digger's life except some smelly recipes. I felt more or less the same way about my relationship with Josh. Corny as it sounds, it was as if what we'd shared had also gone up in smoke, and all I had left was this ugly, stinky mess.

The phone rang, and my stomach dropped. I glared at the caller ID as I waited for the number to appear. It could be Josh, I told myself. Did I want it to be Josh or not? I wasn't sure.

Instead of my ex, the caller was Kyle. I wanted to sound completely nonchalant and to behave as though I had never assaulted him, but instead of staying cool, I found myself rattling off ideas at an auctioneer's pace. "Kyle! Oh, good! Listen, I got ahold of Digger's recipes, and there are tons here that would be perfect for the book, and I really think that we need to use some of them, which reminds me that we absolutely have to start testing the recipes we do have, because you can never trust a chef, and just because a recipe came from a chef doesn't mean that the amounts and proportions of ingredients are right and—"

"Breath!" Kyle demanded with a laugh. "Stop and take a breath! But you're right. We should test the recipes. Why don't you pick out a few, and we can get together and do some cooking."

Obediently, I took a slow breath. Kyle was behaving normally, and I should follow suit. "Great. I have some ideas already."

"Would you mind if we cooked at your place? The apartment I'm renting has a really small galley kitchen, and we'd have a tough time here. I know your place isn't gargantuan, but it's the better of the two options."

"Absolutely. How about Tuesday night? I should be home from my internship by five thirty."

"Why don't you do the food shopping, and then I'll reimburse you in your next check. Oh, and have your friend Adrianna come over if she wants. I'm sure we could use the help, and she seems like she'd give us some honest feedback about the dishes."

"I bet she'd be thrilled. I'll give her a call."

I hung up, started a shopping list, and immediately realized that I was going to blow my entire last paycheck on ingredients. I would get my money back, of course, and I'd charge for every second I spent at the store, but I'd have to go shopping tomorrow night so that we'd have everything we needed for Tuesday. I called Adrianna and Owen, and left a message inviting them over to cook and taste the food with Kyle and me. I was sure they'd take me up on the offer, especially because money was super tight for them these days. In fact, I was seriously worried that they weren't eating well. In particular, since she was still nursing, Ade needed all the sustenance she could get.

Going through recipes and planning Tuesday's cooking projects helped to distract me from dwelling on Josh. Helped. Somewhat. A little. In addition to being broke, I was still a jumpy, frazzled mess, and I gave in to the compulsion to keep checking my e-mail every ten minutes or so until I went to bed. Tomorrow, I assured myself, I'd be at my internship all day and nowhere near my computer. Maybe my supervisor would let me use hers, and I'd be able to check my e-mail from work? No, no! *Josh does not exist. Josh does not exist,* I repeated uselessly.

ELEVEN

I shifted my weight in the uncomfortable armchair and forced myself to look sympathetically at my client Alison. She was exceedingly beautiful, there was no doubt about that, but nutty as a loon. I was midway through my day at my internship—pardon me, my field placement—at the community mental health center and was listening to one of my regular clients drone on about her love life. Alison was a twenty-one-year-old college student who could have had practically any man she chose, yet she had a pattern of falling for unavailable older men. The woes of the young and beautiful, huh? Most of our counseling sessions centered on my trying to get to the root of her relationship issues so that we could figure out why she kept setting herself up to fail in her romantic life. So far we hadn't made much progress, and I increasingly believed that Alison really wanted me to tell her that, yes, it was a brilliant idea for her to devote herself to the married workaholic who thought she had a great ass.

Alison twirled a long spiral curl around her manicured finger and crossed her mile-long legs. She had changed her eye color this week and now flashed violet eyes in my direction. "Ms. Carter?"

"Yes, Alison?"

"I really think that I found the right guy, this time." She smiled, clearly pleased with herself.

I nodded, waiting for her to go on. One of the lessons drilled into us social-work students was that it was sometimes best to say nothing, to wait and see what a client did with silence. Alison usually used these moments as opportunities to announce new affairs.

"Don't you want to hear about him?" she asked eagerly.

"Do you want to tell me about him?" Another social-work strategy: answer a question with a question. If I'd been allowed to be honest, I'd have screamed that hell no, I didn't want to hear about Alison's latest unavailable interest and that I wished she'd just enjoy the normal, loving, college-age boyfriend she had. Then I'd have run screaming from the room. In other words, I desperately needed to work on my patience and to focus on the goal of helping this young woman straighten out her life. Not that I felt like a particularly good role model, having spent the past two days jumping every time the phone rang and daydreaming about fooling around with Josh in the condemned apartment. . . .

"Okay!" Alison sat up straight and clapped her hands.

"His name is Keith, and he's totally gorgeous. Older than me, obviously, because you know I have a thing for mature men. But he's not, like, ancient or anything. I think he's about forty-five. Totally suave and sexy. He was a guest lecturer in my friend's college class, and he's written books and makes awesome money." She rubbed her fingers together and lifted an eyebrow. "I met him through my friend after he took a group of students out to dinner, and he invited me along because I was outside talking to her when he asked. I think she might be a little into him, but he obviously is much more attracted to me. I can tell we like each other, even though we haven't said anything."

I cleared my throat. This story was not screaming *appropriate*. A middle-aged man taking young college students out to dinner? Please. "You do already have a boyfriend, though. Tom. How is that relationship going for you? And do you think this new man, Keith, is the kind of man you could have a relationship with?"

She shrugged happily. "Keith is well traveled, smart, sexy. . . . Did I already say sexy? Well, he is. A real gentleman, too. He holds doors open for women, and he's really nice to all of my friends. Tom is such a bore compared to him. I mean, there's nothing wrong with him, but he's not what I really want. I wish Keith would just whisk me away to some tropical paradise where we could lounge around and sip cocktails and get massages."

I was hoping to guide Alison toward the realization that her choices in boyfriends usually led to disastrous results. Who knew if this older man was even interested in her? There was a strong possibility that she'd conjured up the romance. It was even possible that the man existed entirely in her head.

I spent another forty minutes questioning Alison about her attraction to this man and making notes as we talked. *A has expressed interest in older, suave gentleman K and is considering abandoning current relationship, claiming relationship is a "bore." Impressed with K's world experience and has fantasy that he reciprocates her attraction.*

When my session with Alison was over, I grabbed a quick lunch and checked my voice mail on both my cell phone and my home phone. No calls from Josh, but one from Kyle confirming our night of recipe testing.

My next client, Danny, was someone I really liked. He was my age, twenty-six, and worked long hours in construction. His father owned the company and, according to Danny, was a real bastard, a demeaning, tyrannical man who subjected his son to one harsh criticism after another. Claiming that it was for his son's own good, the father demanded that Danny work twice as hard as the other workers to prove himself to his father. In my opinion, Danny was no more than a slave to his father, yet Danny killed himself to live up to his father's standards.

Today my client showed up with his entire left hand wrapped thickly with gauze. "Danny, what happened?" I asked.

Danny smiled and waved away my concern. "Ah, it's nothin'. I just got hurt a few days ago." He leaned back in his chair and wiped his forehead with the back of his hand. His curly black hair was damp with sweat, and his ruddy cheeks were flushed from working outside in the cold all morning. To get to our appointments, Danny told his father that he was taking a business class. He'd never have let his father know that he was going to therapy. "Therapy is for sissies," the father had told Danny.

I eyed Danny's hand. "That looks serious."

"Nah. I cut myself with an electric saw. Just a nick really. My dad had me wrap it up, and I went to the ER after my shift."

"What time did this happen?"

"First thing in the morning. Can you believe it? What a way to start of the day, huh?"

"And you usually work from six in the morning until four thirty in the afternoon?"

Danny nodded as he looked at his bandaged hand.

"So your father wouldn't let you go to the emergency room for what? Eight hours?"

Danny nodded again. "I needed fourteen stitches." He hung his head. "But I wanted him to know that I could tough it out. That I'm the son he always wanted. And it's not like it didn't stop bleeding or anything. I wrapped it myself and it was fine." He laughed softly. "It's nothing new, though. I get hurt all the time. You know, when I was a kid, there were two bullies who lived up the block from us. One time they beat the crap out of me. I was ten, and these kids just pummeled me. For no reason whatsoever. Just because they were assholes. And they thought I was a loser. I mean, I was a scrawny, funny-looking kid, but I never did anything to them. The older one broke my cheekbone, he hit me so hard."

I never would have guessed that Danny had ever been

less than the strapping, handsome man who sat in front of me. I wished that I could sic him on those bullies today. "What was your father's response when you came home so injured?"

"He smacked me on the back of the head and told me it would make me a man." Danny paused. "And he said I better not cry or he'd finish what the kids started."

"Oh, Danny."

"When my Dad went out later that afternoon, my mother took me to the hospital. But I didn't cry once." He forced a smile. "When I was healing and all black-and-blue, my dad would point out my bruises to his friends and act all proud of me. Like I was worthy of being his son because I'd been in a fight. Not that I'd done much fighting back, but he didn't know that. Look, I'm making it sound worse than it was. My dad really wants the best for me. And he's right that I need to be motivated. I can be really lazy, and I need to be pushed sometimes. He wants me to be big-time, you know? Take over his company one day."

It took all of my willpower to control my breathing. I hated hearing stories like Danny's, which were all too common. I wanted Danny to quit his job and move far away from the father he'd been stuck with, but it was important to help him start making decisions for himself and eventually to realize on his own that his father was abusive. My client's pattern of driving himself to the ground to impress his father had to end. As Danny continued to talk, I took notes, in part to be able to review them later and in part to keep busy and distance myself as I listened to yet more examples of his father's destructive behavior. To continue to do clinical work, I'd have to learn to tolerate hearing painful stories, but so far, I found the experience almost overwhelming.

By the time I got off work, I was drained and depressed. What's more, I was ashamed. Listening to my clients had reminded me that there were much worse things in life than a broken heart. Unlike some of my clients, I had a wonderful, loving family and close friends. Still, I had to acknowledge that even with a healthy upbringing and a stable family system, I had a right to feel upset about Josh. The experts, including the professor who taught my class on attachment, would agree that I was mourning the loss of a relationship and needed to grieve.

It was pitch-black when I got back to my condo. I cursed November's early sunsets. The dark seemed to exacerbate depression and make bad moods worse. I briefly considered investing in some sort of bright light to shine on my face; my breakup had probably given me a case of seasonal affective disorder. I let myself in the back door and dropped my notepad on the coffee table. I hadn't yet typed up today's client notes and was hoping to have time to complete the task after the recipe-testing dinner party. In fact, because of client confidentiality, I was probably supposed to have left the notes in my office, but I'd wanted to get home as quickly as possible to get ready for Kyle, Adrianna, and Owen. Cooking would be fun and, especially after the day I'd had, my spirits needed lifting

Danny's situation was still hanging over me. When I'd talked to my supervisor about him, she'd reminded me that change happens slowly. Even though it was obvious to me that Danny needed to stand up to his father and make decisions for himself, it would take time before he was ready. She reminded me that some cases were inevitably more gut-wrenching than others: for every eye-rolling Alison, there would be a Danny. I was impatient, though, and the urge to rescue him was powerful.

I fed Gato and Inga, and gave them some cuddles before reviewing the dishes we'd be making tonight. I had two of Digger's recipes, the one for stromboli and another for pork tenderloin with cranberry glaze, smoked bacon mashed pota-toes, and celery root slaw. I'd also chosen a few other recipes from Kyle's research: a pan-seared swordfish with butternut squash risotto, a ragout of Brussels sprouts and wild mush-rooms, and a dessert called aloha fruit salad. I'd chosen the salad because Owen, whose cooking skills were more than limited, could help to prepare it without having the oppor-tunity to burn anything. Adrianna and I were solid cooks, and Kyle could presumably hold his own in the kitchen. The combination of dishes was strange, but they wouldn't all be grouped together in the cookbook as a suggested menu, which we'd have to keep in mind when tasting them.

I started the stromboli dough, which had to rise for at least an hour. Kyle arrived just as I was setting it in a bowl. He waved at me though the glass window on the back door, and I yelled for him to let himself in. When I smiled and held up my dough-covered hands, he smiled back. Good. Maybe things between us wouldn't be horribly awkward. For all I knew, he'd even appreciated my enthusiastic, if clumsy, attempt at romance. Tonight could be a romantic evening for all of us. Two couples in the kitchen, whipping up delicious food, maybe sipping some wine. . . .

Contemplating the possibilities, I struggled to push the Josh situation to the back of my mind. Amazingly, I hadn't told Adrianna about seeing Josh. Since Ade and I always told each other everything, usually as soon as possible and at great length, it was very unlike me not to have immediately called her up after the emotional reunion. On this occasion, however, I just hadn't wanted to deal with my feelings about Josh, and a big two-hour talk with Ade about my turbulent emotions and the implications of seeing him would only have made the mess more real. The new Chloe was forging ahead!

"What are you making, Chloe?" Kyle was dressed casually tonight in a pale blue fitted shirt and jeans. I realized that it was the first time that I'd seen him in anything other than a suit. I wasn't complaining either.

"Stromboli dough," I said. "I thought I'd get it going early since we've got so much to do."

Kyle followed me into the kitchen, where I showed him the recipes we were going to make.

"These all look really good," he said. "I'm glad you were able to get hold of your friend Digger's recipes, too. We'll do a nice section on him. I'm sorry again about how my father behaved the morning of the fire. He's just very focused on getting this book done right, and he wasn't thinking about anything else."

"I'm happy about the food, too. This stromboli is Digger's, so I'm sure it'll be good."

"So Adrianna is helping us out tonight, too?" Kyle sat down at my small kitchen table, but I immediately grabbed his hand and lifted him up.

"Yes, help will be here shortly," I promised. "You're in charge of washing vegetables, so roll up your sleeves."

"Aw, really? That's not exciting. I was hoping to be in charge of searing and roasting and sautéing!" He feigned a pout and then smiled. "If you insist."

I opened the refrigerator and began covering the countertop with produce. The ingredients for all of tonight's dishes had come with such a hefty price tag that I hoped Kyle wouldn't faint when he saw the receipt. Kyle began scrubbing celery root while I located an assortment of mixing bowls, sauté pans, knives, and cutting boards. I'd acquired a lot of decent cooking equipment over the past year, mostly because I'd been embarrassed to have Josh try to cook in my house with lousy stuff.

At least the good knives hadn't followed him to Hawaii.

TWELVE

I heard the back door open when Ade and Owen let themselves in.

"We're here and ready to follow orders," Ade called as her high heels clicked across the floor.

She came into the kitchen, carrying Patrick close to her body in a Snugli. No one but Adrianna could manage heels that high and a baby, too. Patrick must have been sleeping well, I thought, because she looked rested. Her thick blonde hair was flawlessly styled, and she'd made up her eyes in smoky gray eyeliner and heavy black mascara. I had a strong suspicion that I wouldn't look nearly so glamorous if I had a three-month-old. But that was Adrianna for you: she could survive a tornado and emerge sultry and sexy. If Adrianna had flaunted her looks, I might have been filled with envy, but she remained so oblivious to how attractive she was that I couldn't hold her spectacular beauty against her.

"Hi, Kyle. Chloe's got you working already? Tough boss, huh?" Adrianna winked at him and laughed.

"Hey!" I protested as I set a ceramic bowl on the table. "I'm just trying to be organized about this. We've got a lot of work to do and not that much space, so we have to go at this with a game plan. I've got the timeline all worked out." I rubbed Patrick's feet and grinned at his sleepy face.

"Well, Patrick just ate, so he should go to sleep for a while. Owen is just setting up the Pack 'n Play in Chloe's bedroom."

"I didn't realize Owen would be here, too," Kyle said over the whoosh of the faucet. "I finally get to meet him."

"Yes, but don't let him cook anything," Ade warned. "Last night we had hamburgers that were burned on the outside and still mooing on the inside." She wrinkled her nose. "We had to finish them off in the oven, but that didn't help the burned taste."

Kyle moved the celery root to the side and started peeling some of the fruit for the salad. "Adrianna, do you want to start the squash?"

"Sure. Let me just set Patrick down and I'll be right there."

A few minutes later Owen tiptoed into the kitchen. "The little man is out like the proverbial light. And I am ready to cook!"

I raised my eyebrows at Owen. He had on one of his awful T-shirts, the one that was supposed to look like a tuxedo top, and on his head was a towering red-and-white-striped felt hat. The Cat in the Hat had come to dinner. I giggled and shook my head at Owen. "Thank God Adrianna is around to dress Patrick. If you were in charge, who knows what the poor kid might be wearing?"

"Patrick is lucky to have me as a role model. All of us need a little Dr. Seuss in our lives." Owen bowed dramatically.

"Even in that outfit, you still look adorable." I gave him a kiss on the cheek. "And yes, there is something to be said for Seussing up one's life, but at least I got you to cut out your attempt at duplicating his style in your wedding vows!"

Owen rolled his eyes as Adrianna came up behind him and wrapped an arm around his waist. She looked at Kyle and explained. "We wrote our own vows, and Chloe performed our wedding ceremony. My dear husband had the audacity to write his vows to the beat of Dr. Seuss. Chloe had to practically throttle him until he agreed to go a more traditional route."

"Hey, it would have been funny!" Owen stuck out his lower lip. "So, you must be Kyle?" He stepped toward my boss and stuck out his hand. "I've heard so much about you. Thanks for treating Adrianna to dinner the other night. She said she had a wonderful time. Not as good as my burgers, but a close second."

Kyle laughed. "I'm glad. It's nice to meet you, too." He shook Owen's hand politely, but I could see that he was taking in Owen's eccentric attire.

"So, where do you want us?" Owen looked around my cramped kitchen.

"I think it might make sense to send you and Kyle into

the living room. You can prep all the vegetables and fruit that we'll need there. Just move whatever's on the coffee table onto a chair. Here," I said, reaching behind my toaster, "take this cutting board and the two from the table. Kyle, is everything washed?"

"Yup, just about." Kyle handed Owen a colander filled with ingredients and then grabbed the stack of bowls I'd set out for him. "We'll chop, slice, and dice, and be ready in no time."

"And, here, take this." I gave Kyle a large serving bowl that held the ingredients for the aloha salad dressing. "Ade and I will work on the stromboli filling, the pork loin, and the swordfish."

"Hey, Chloe?" Kyle said softly.

"Yeah?"

"Thanks for doing all of this. I know you have a lot going on with school and your internship, and maybe this job is more than you bargained for. But I'm really grateful for your help." He followed Owen to the makeshift prep station in the living room.

"Well, well." Adrianna shot me a questioning look. Almost whispering, she asked, "What's going on between you two?"

I shook my head. "Nothing," I murmured. "He's my boss."

"Yeah, right," she said with a laugh. "We'll talk later."

Adrianna was great in the kitchen. In particular, she helped me follow the recipes exactly as they were written; if we improvised, we'd be playing with the recipes rather than testing them. So far, I'd found no glaring errors in what the chefs had written, and I expected tonight's dishes to be successful. Adrianna talked about Patrick: he was growing so quickly and doing something new every day. We could hear Owen and Kyle talking in the background, and I was pleased that the two were getting along so well. This was a fun foursome we had tonight. Maybe it would become a regular thing?

"Chloe, do you want to come taste this dressing?" Kyle called.

I joined the men and surveyed their progress. Bowls were spread out on the table, and they'd done pretty well slicing and dicing the ingredients. Then I eyed the bowl of dressing that Kyle held out. "Oh my. That's quite a bit of dressing."

"Yeah, the recipe made a large amount, but it's good. I actually ran out of lemons to juice, but it's good anyway."

I saw Owen's eyes widen as I dipped a spoon into the bowl and took a taste. Oh God! I puckered my lips. "It's rather . . . acidic."

"You think? I like it. I followed the recipe. Look," he said as he held out the typed page. "Oh, wait. Oops. I thought it said three cups of lemon juice."

"That would explain it. It's supposed to be one-third cup of lemon juice." I smiled falsely. "No problem. I have a few more lemons in the fridge, so we can make another batch." I retrieved the lemons and handed them to Owen, hoping that he'd get the hint to keep an eye on Kyle. I laughed inwardly at the idea of putting Owen in charge of anything even remotely related to cooking, but clearly Kyle needed supervision, and even Owen wouldn't use three cups of lemon juice when a recipe called for a third of a cup. I could hardly believe that anyone, never mind a cookbook writer and Hank Boucher's son, had failed to notice the overwhelming taste of lemon in the dressing. Worse, Kyle had told me that the dressing was good! What kind of palate did he have? Ugh. Did he have a palate at all?

Despite the dressing mishap, I was having a good time. Adrianna was putting the pork loin into the oven and I was just about to fill the stromboli dough when the phone rang. "Hello, Chaos Central!" I chirped happily.

"Hi." There was a long pause. "It's me."

My stomach tightened and I swallowed hard. It was the call I'd been both longing for and dreading. It was Josh. He must have gotten my new cell number from someone. I strongly suspected Ade or Owen. "Oh. Hi."

"How you doin'?" The sound of his voice practically knocked the wind out of me.

"Um . . . fine." I saw that Adrianna was staring at me. I could feel my cheeks heat up and wondered whether my best friend could hear my heart pounding. "Hold on a second." I went into the hallway. I couldn't go to the living room, where Owen and Kyle would overhear, or to the bedroom, where Patrick was sleeping. That left the bathroom. As I stepped onto the tile floor, Kyle let out a sharp cry. "Are you okay?" I called.

"Yeah," Kyle answered. "Just nicked myself, that's all."

"Josh?" I said into the phone.

"Yeah. You've obviously got someone there. Sorry to have bothered you," he said quickly. "I'll talk to you later."

"No, wait! Don't go!" I pleaded uselessly after he'd hung

up. I shut my eyes and took a breath before going back to the kitchen.

Adrianna set the timer on the oven and turned to me. "Anything you want to tell me, pal?"

As my eyes started to well up, Ade took me into a tight hug. "That was Josh, wasn't it?" she asked. I nodded and she squeezed me tighter.

"I saw him on Sunday. At Digger's." I gave her a whispered rundown of the surprise encounter. "I'm trying to pretend this isn't happening."

"I know it hurts," she whispered in my ear. "I know how much you love him."

"Loved him," I corrected her and pulled away. "He heard Kyle. He probably thinks . . . well, he heard him."

"Is that what you want him to think?"

"Yes." I paused. "No. I shouldn't play games, and there's nothing going on with Kyle. Well, not really." I described my ludicrous attempt to make out with Kyle in his car. "I just don't think it's happening with us. I don't know if I even want it to."

"Look, for now, let's get through tonight and enjoy dinner. Whether or not you and Kyle have anything, he's a nice guy, and we'll have fun. You can deal with Josh later. Come on, let's go check on the boys."

The four of us worked well as a team, especially because Owen and Kyle were willing to follow our orders blindly. The food was fabulous. Because we had two main dishes as well as the stromboli and the fruit salad, the meal was more an uncoordinated tasting experience than it was a dinner, but everyone got into the spirit and lavished praise on the chefs who had created the recipes. I was sure that Digger would have been pleased with our attempts to recreate his dishes. The stromboli was so hot that steam flew out of the dough as I tore off pieces for all of us. After the honey-pineapple-lemon dressing had been remade, we all enjoyed the delicious salad of mango, apple, banana, orange, coconut, dates, and macadamia nuts.

We ate in the living room with our plates on our laps or on the coffee table, but the tight dining quarters didn't bother us. "With food this great, I don't care where we eat," Ade said as she bit into a piece of swordfish. "You've got more room here then we do at our place, Chloe, so this feels like a mansion."

"Yeah, I know we're cramped right now, hon," Owen said. "Things will get better."

Ade shrugged. "We'll see. This fish business of yours isn't doing so well, though. How long should we give it?"

Ade had pushed a button with her husband. Owen rarely got irritated, but his face tensed visibly. "Let's hang on a bit longer. I'm still working to get in good with restaurants and to get the chefs to trust that I'll bring them the best product."

"Whatever," Ade said rather coolly.

Patrick, who'd awakened midway through our meal, was now in the crook of Adrianna's arm, gazing admiringly at his mother. Adrianna, seated on the floor, leaned back and rested a hand on the rug. "I think this cookbook is going to hit the best-seller list. Keep working, you two, so we can come back and taste test more recipes. I haven't eaten this well since, well, since Kyle took us out," she said with a laugh.

"Yeah, how do I get in on this dining-out gig?" Owen asked as he adjusted his striped hat.

"Anytime," Kyle answered, but he was staring at Patrick. "You two make quite a pair," he said, looking at Adrianna. "Patrick looks very happy and comfortable."

"Do you want to have kids?" Owen asked.

"Definitely." Kyle began clearing dishes. "If I didn't before, Patrick would have changed my mind."

"You're seeing him at his best, though," Ade said. "You might change your mind if you heard him screaming his brains out at two thirty in the morning."

"Aw, he's a great baby," Kyle said. "I'll start washing dishes so poor Chloe isn't stuck with too much to do herself." He surprised me by tousling my hair as he walked by me.

"Thanks. I'll start packing up the leftovers. Everyone is going home with food for the rest of the week, I think."

I scrounged around for whatever storage containers I could find. Since it was pointless to try to find matching lids, most of the containers got covered in plastic wrap. Owen put away pots and pans while Adrianna got Patrick ready to go home. Because they lived only a few blocks away, they'd walked over, but in addition to the baby and all of his gear, they now had leftovers to carry and were laden down.

"Why don't I drive Owen home, and he can get the car and come back for you and Patrick and all of your stuff?" I suggested.

"Nah, it's only a few blocks. We'll be fine," Ade said, but she glanced at her high heels.

"I'll walk them back," Kyle offered. "I'd drive you, except that I assume you need a car seat for the baby. I should get going anyway." He turned to me. "Chloe, thanks again for hosting this evening. And please bill us for all of the hours you spent preparing for tonight and for this evening. Great work. I'll talk to you in a few days, and we'll figure out our next step."

"Sure." I tried to look cheery. So much for any romantic intentions on Kyle's part. I had half expected him to hang around after my friends left, but we were apparently all business. Still, it was thoughtful of him to help Owen and Ade out. "Things are pretty well cleaned up here, and I should be getting to bed. I have another long day at my field placement tomorrow."

Ade and Owen hugged me good-bye, and Ade promised to call me the next day. Kyle took my hand in his and politely kissed me on the cheek, thanking me again for all of my help. Suddenly, my condo was empty and disturbingly quiet. I'd been alone for only a few minutes when the emptiness overwhelmed me. I wanted nothing more than for Josh to call back. It didn't matter how many people I crammed into my condo or how much fun we had or how temporarily distracted I got. The truth was that I missed Josh so much that it hurt. I picked the phone up and started to dial his number, but stopped just before I hit the Talk button.

I set the phone back into the cradle and got ready for bed.

THIRTEEN

I dragged myself up the stairs after a tough day at the mental health center. Especially because I was drained, it was an incredible relief to see Adrianna sitting in front of my door. She handed me a coffee in a foam cup.

"Thank God," I said. "How'd you know I needed you and caffeine, in that order?"

Ade stretched out her hand, and I lifted her up. "I know this Josh thing has you shook up. Thought you could use a friend. Besides, Owen is home reading to Patrick, so I thought I'd escape the house for a bit."

After I unlocked the door, turned on a few lights, and threw the mail on the coffee table, we both headed for the couch. "He's reading to him? How cute!"

Ade snorted. "Yeah, he's reading from a seafood ency-clopedia. Patrick loves it. He stares at his daddy. One day he'll be fussier about what books he listens to, but for now he loves the sound of Owen's voice, and he couldn't care less about the literary subject matter." She grinned. "Owen is the best. I can't imagine a better father."

I kicked off my shoes and sank into the cushion. "I'm so happy for you. I was going to ask if everything was all right between you two. There seemed to be a little tension last night over his job and the apartment."

"Oh, that," she said dismissively. "Yeah, his job is sort of crappy, and we'd love to live in a big fat house in the suburbs, but I'm nuts about him. I really am. And you know," she said as she leaned into me, "we were pretty damn happy when we got the doctor's okay to have sex again. Let me tell you, no one wants to have sex when she's humongously pregnant. And then, after the delivery? Please, I thought that no one was ever getting close to that region again. Who knew? Now that we're both get-tin' some lovin' . . . Well, it's a happy household." Ade got such a dreamy look on her face that I couldn't help laughing.

"I'm glad to hear it, but considering that I think of Owen as a brother, I'll pass on any graphic details."

"I think you just don't want to know because you're not getting any yourself."

"Hey!"

"Well, it's true. Or maybe you're not ready?"

"I'm ready." I scooped up Gato and sat him on my lap. "Ready-ish."

"Liar! You are so not over Josh." Ade smirked happily. "Good."

"Good? It's not good. It sucks. I hate to admit that I'm not over him. After he totally ditched me and flew off to Hawaii? I can't still be in love with him."

"But you are," Ade said gently. "And from what you've told me about that hot-and-heavy make-out session you two had the other day, I'd say he's still in love with you."

"Josh only came back to Boston because he thinks Digger's death was a murder." I ran my hands through my hair and sighed. "He didn't come back for me."

"Actually, I don't know if that's true. Josh called me today," Ade confessed. "He wanted to know what you thought was going on with Digger before he died."

"He called you?"

"Yup. He was in a rotten mood. Partly because of Digger, partly because he's staying with Snacker, whose girlfriend is there all the time, and partly because of you."

"What did he say about me? What did he say?" I demanded.

"He didn't have to say anything, Chloe. I know Josh pretty well, and I know that he was fishing for details. Asking me how you were, what you've been up to, that kind of thing."

"Did he say anything about hearing Kyle last night when he called?"

"No, not specifically, but he wouldn't ask about you if he didn't still care. I could hear it in his voice." Adrianna cocked her head to side and looked at me. "Chloe? Why didn't you go to Hawaii with Josh?"

"What?"

"Why didn't you go to Hawaii?"

I rolled my eyes. "Ade! People don't just drop their lives and run off to Hawaii for the hell of it."

"It wouldn't have been for the hell of it. It would have been for you. For you and Josh."

"I have responsibilities. School, for one. My whole family is in Boston. And there's you and Owen and Patrick. I wasn't about to leave all of you," I insisted. "Oh my God! You think I should have gone."

She shrugged. "You said no awfully quickly."

"He asked awfully quickly," I spat back. "He asked me to go with him and left the next day."

"True. But you could have met up with him. You didn't have to leave that minute. And there are other graduate schools in the country, including in Hawaii, I'll bet, and plane rides home and phone calls and e-mails."

"I cannot believe you. So you wouldn't have cared if I'd just left?"

"Of course I would have cared, dummy. I would miss you like crazy. We all would. But you and I will always be best friends, no matter where you are."

"Hawaii is not exactly an option now, is it? I said no, and we broke up. What's done is done."

"It's not done yet, Chloe," Ade said as she put her hand on my arm. "You don't get that many chances at truly mind-blowing romance. I almost lost Owen once, and I thank God every day that I didn't. He is without a doubt the love of my life. And I think Josh might be yours."

"Well, he's not. Stop talking like we're fated to be together or some nonsense like that. More important than my stupid love life is what happened to Digger. So, Josh is asking around about him? I only had one short phone call with Digger a few days before he died, and I didn't get the sense that anything was wrong. I mean, sure, he was working like crazy to get the restaurant ready to open, but that's nothing unusual. The only weird thing that's happened is that his girlfriend, Ellie, was all heartbroken and depressed about Digger's death one minute and then furious and hateful about him the next. Somebody else might know more, but I hadn't really been in touch with Digger since Josh left. Division of friends and all that. You can tell Josh that."

"Tell him yourself." Ade winked at me and set her coffee down. "I'm starving. Got anything to eat?"

"Yeah, help yourself," I said distractedly.

Adrianna got up to get us a snack, and I poked through the mail. I couldn't believe that Josh had called Adrianna. She was my best friend, and he knew damn well that she'd tell me about their phone call. I set aside a few bills to pay and scanned a menu for a new Vietnamese restaurant that had just opened. There was also a formal-looking envelope that had my name and address practically embossed in red lettering. I ripped it open, wondering whether someone I knew was getting married. The ivory note card inside, which was covered in the same fancy lettering as the envelope, turned out to be an invitation to the opening of the Penthouse. The date was the coming Friday: short notice. But Digger's death must have thrown a major wrench into the restaurant's plans. I dropped the invitation in my lap. Ellie had obviously put me on the guest list, and my name hadn't been removed after Digger's death. Well, I was always happy to support a new restaurant, and the food was sure to be good; Digger had presumably been replaced with someone equally gifted in the kitchen.

I looked more closely at the invitation to see who the new executive chef was. Jason Freelin. It took me a second to place the name. Although I actually knew Jason Freelin, no one ever called him that. He was known only as Snacker. So, Josh's old (well, now temporarily current) roommate and former sous-chef at Simmer had taken over for Digger! I was amazed, mystified, and skeptical. I mean, I loved Snacker. He was funny, charming, and charismatic, and he really was a wonderful friend to Josh and a great cook. But as the title suggests, an executive chef needs to have exactly the kind of executive ability that Snacker lacked. I simply could not picture Snacker mustering the skill to lead an entire staff and to run the whole business end of the kitchen at a large restaurant. Executive ability must've been why Digger got the job in the first place; besides being talented, he was tough, disciplined, and organized. Yeah, he swore all the time and had a bit of a temper, but he knew how to take charge, and he could get the job done. Snacker, on the other hand, was more likely to flirt with hot waitresses than he was to do inventory or to prepare for health department inspections.

When Adrianna set a plate down on the table, I suddenly realized how hungry I was. She'd put together some cheese, crackers, olives, and slices of sopresatta. "Yum!" I smeared some creamy goat cheese onto a cracker and showed Ade the invitation. "Check out who got Digger's job."

Adrianna scanned the note card. "Who the hell is Jason Freelin?"

"You made out with him and you don't know his name? That's Snacker."

"You have to be kidding me. When would he have time to run a restaurant, what with all the flirting he's got to fit into his day? I feel sorry for that Georgie girl. Snacker can't be the best boyfriend out there."

"Wait, what?" I spoke through a mouthful of food. "Did you say Georgie?"

Ade nodded. "Yeah, Josh mentioned her name to me. Why? Do you know her?"

Of course. Georgie was Ellie's friend, the one I'd called to be with Ellie after I'd broken the news about Digger. Ellie had called Georgie's boyfriend Jay. Aha! Jay had to be short for Jason. Only a girlfriend could get away with calling Snacker by anything close to his real name. One of the women, Ellie or Georgie, must have introduced the other to Digger or to Snacker. Digger and Snacker were old friends who'd been competing for the same job at the Penthouse. I explained the foursome to Adrianna.

"I bet Digger kept Snacker in line with Georgie. Digger seemed like a good guy. I hope Snacker wasn't too pissed off at him for beating him out for the job."

"Well . . . what if he was? You don't think Snacker would . . . you know?" I ran my finger across my throat.

"Don't you think for one minute that Snacker killed Digger! Are you insane?"

"I know you and Snacker had your little thing a while back, but it doesn't mean you have to scream at me for thinking out loud." I crossed my arms and glared at her.

"First of all, stop referring to my poorly chosen little dalliance with Snacker. It was nothing but a few hot kisses here and there, and it was a stupid, horrible mistake, and I'm lucky Owen forgave me for it. But, by the way"—she leaned toward me—"he is a fantastic kisser. Not too much tongue, strong lips. So if things don't happen with Josh or Kyle, you might want to look his way."

"Now who's gone insane?" I playfully pushed her away. "Look, if Josh thinks that someone killed Digger, then it's worth thinking about. What Josh said was that Digger was a professional chef who'd never have done something careless at home that could start a kitchen fire."

"So you're suggesting that Snacker killed Digger to get his job? Snacker was already the sous-chef there, right? Why would he want more responsibility? You know how he is, Chloe. He's a goof. Yes, he's probably fooling around on poor Georgie, so fine, maybe you could call him disloyal and opportunistic, but he didn't murder anyone. Who else could have wanted Digger out of the picture?"

"There's this neighbor of Digger's, Norris, who actually seemed relieved that he didn't have to live next door to Digger anymore." I told Ade about Norris's litany of complaints against the chef. "And why is Ellie suddenly so bullshit at her dead boyfriend? I have no idea what that's about."

"So you've got a chef, a neighbor, and a girlfriend to investigate now."

"Josh started this, so blame him. And stop hogging the Brie."

FOURTEEN

"I'LL take it," I said to the salesgirl. I smoothed my hands down the luxurious fabric and checked myself out in the three-way mirror. Josh could eat his heart out when he saw me. He was bound to be at the restaurant opening on Friday, and there was no way I was wearing something less than spectacular to the event. And this form-fitting navy number was exactly what I needed to make a smashing entrance. It was Thursday, and I had a two-hour break between classes in the middle of the day, giving me enough time to shop before my supervision class.

"It really suits you perfectly." The salesgirl nodded her approval. "Are you going somewhere special?"

I'm going to see my ex, and I need to look like a sexy love vixen and make him drop to the floor, overwhelmed by his stupidity for ever leaving me. "Just a restaurant opening tomorrow."

"Well, you'll look great. Do you have a nice coat to go with this? You can't throw any old winter coat over this designer piece." She frowned at the contemptible image.

Twenty minutes later, I left the upscale shop with the dress and a matching faux-fur-lined coat. More purchases to pay off, but it would be worth it. I called Kyle from the car. "Did you get your invitation to the Penthouse's opening on Friday? I thought maybe we could go together. Adrianna and Owen are going, too. I called to RSVP and managed to get Ade and Owen in with me."

"You bet. It looks great. But do you think it'll upset you because of your friend Digger? It was supposed to be his opening."

"I think it's important for me to be there for his sake. Besides, I know Snacker, who's taken over as the executive chef, and I'm sure he could use the support." I failed to mention my intention to pass Kyle off as my date in front of Josh, but Kyle didn't need to know everything.

"Why don't I pick you all up at seven on Friday night?" Kyle offered.

"Wonderful. And I'm making excellent progress on the book. I can update you at the opening." It was a small lie. My progress on the book wasn't exactly *excellent*, but there were only so many recipes that I could test myself. I had to fight to fit in classes, homework, and cookbook work, and I certainly didn't have the energy or the drive to stay up until three in the morning cooking delicacies. There was just too much testing for one person to accomplish, and

I'd been brainstorming about whom to enlist to help me. I could probably get my parents and my sister to test a few recipes, but even with their help, the amount of work felt overwhelming.

I loaded my bags in the car and headed back to school. The supervision group was my least hateful class, so I wasn't dreading this afternoon as much as I dreaded the rest of school. It was a small class, made up of ten students and one teacher, and we met in one of the comfortable lounges on campus, where we all got to spread out on couches and cushy chairs and sip coffee from one of the vending carts. This class was our opportunity to present our cases to our peers and to get feedback on our performance and input from others about treatment options. Somehow, it felt sort of gossipy to trade stories about other people's lives, but I admit that I enjoyed hearing other students' anecdotes. Slipping into the lounge just as the professor was about to shut the door, I grabbed the end seat on my favorite couch.

I listened to students present several cases that made mine look like a walk in the psychotherapeutic park. Julie was doing her field placement in the foster-care system, a setting that not only required her to navigate a nightmare tangle of red tape, but also involved challenging, emotionally demanding client work as well. Robert and Ann Marie were both at a geriatric home, and Simon was working at a community outreach program for teens. When it was my turn to present, I pulled my case files out of my folder and set them on my lap. I also had handy a rather sizeable stack of recipes that had to be tested. The recipes didn't exactly need supervision, but should there happen to be any volunteers . . .

"So, Chloe, tell us about this week's session with Ms. A."
Professor Ruiz adjusted his nearly invisible glasses and crossed
his legs, raising his pant legs to reveal mismatched socks.

We never used clients' real names. Instead, we referred
to a client by the first letter of the person's first name, or we
made up a name. Julie always named her clients after celebrities. We'd spent last week's class hearing all about "Bono's"
struggle to find a loving foster family to take him in. The
week before it had been "Mark Wahlberg's" suspension from
high school for smoking pot in the girls' room. My professor
had cut Julie off when she'd launched into a speech about
how poor "Colin Powell" had caught gonorrhea from "Bruce
Springsteen." I just stuck to letter names.

I scanned my notes. "Well, Ms. A continues to remain
unsatisfied in her current relationship with T. She claims he
is dull and unexciting, and she now has her sights set on a
professor who is more than twice her age. It's my impression
that she may have concocted his attraction to her and that
she has created a romantic connection between herself and
the professor as a way to escape her reality. Her current boyfriend actually sounds like a really decent guy who adores
her, and I wonder if she has fabricated a relationship with
this new man as a way to avoid intimacy." I paused. "As a
way to protect herself from getting hurt." The picture I was
painting suddenly started to sound all too familiar. I hadn't
deluded myself into believing that I had a romantic relationship with Kyle, but there was, I had to admit, a genuine
possibility that, in fantasizing about him, I was avoiding
real intimacy. "Um, let me move on to D, whose father continues to put unreasonable demands on him leading D to

push himself further and further to impress his father. An impossible task, if you ask me. I cannot get D to see that he needs to recognize his own wishes and goals and not to live his life according to this asshole's . . . er, excuse me . . . the unreasonable paternal expectations." When I shared Danny's hand injury with the class, everyone was as visibly horrified as I was. Shared. In supervision, we were encouraged not simply to describe or report or tell things; rather, we were supposed to *share* them. "And yet, even with incidents like that, D continues to want to please his father."

Julie whipped out a pencil, stood up, and paced the floor in front of me. "I think there is an important angle to look at here. Let me take a guess. The more this father pushes his son, the more the son screws up, correct?"

"Yes, actually, that's true." I nodded emphatically.

"Okay, so D's image of his father is one of an important, successful, almighty power, essentially. That only serves to increase the son's sense of incompetence, thereby making him genuinely incompetent. Like the accident with his hand? Probably a result of his nerves and his fear of failure. He'll never feel whole and develop positive self-esteem until he stops believing everything his father says." Julie sat back down, clearly pleased with her insight.

"You're right," I said. "But how in the world do I help him see what's so obvious to us?"

Professor Ruiz leaned forward, intertwined his fingers, and looked thoughtfully at me. "If I were D, I would be pretty angry at my father. But it sounds like your client has turned that anger onto himself. See if you can get him to acknowledge that feeling. It's okay to love someone and also hate some of the person's behavior and words. That's a tough dichotomy to balance, but we are allowed to have mixed feelings about the important people in our lives."

There's a fine line between love and hate. I thought of Josh. I was furious with him for leaving me, of course, but Adrianna had been right when she'd said that I still loved him. Damn. Why couldn't I just be done with him and let that relationship go? There were other men in the world, right?

But there was only one Josh.

"Oh, while I'm here," I said as nonchalantly as possible, "and since I really appreciate all the help the group has given me this semester, I thought of a way to thank everybody. I'm working on a cookbook with a very famous chef, and I've brought some of the secret recipes that will be in the book." I stood up and began handing out sheets of paper to the mystified students. "Julie, you look like a tiramisu girl, am I right?"

"I guess so," she said.

"Come on. It'll be fun," I begged.

"I like to cook," Robert said. "What else do you have?"

"Open ravioli with spinach, tomato, and cream?"

"Yup, that's mine." Robert snatched the paper out of my hands.

"So you all get to test a recipe for the book, and your names will be in the acknowledgments. Isn't this cool?" I said enthusiastically. "Simon, how about I give you lamb? And for you, Ann Marie? Chicken Creole!"

"I love anything Creole." Ann Marie rubbed her stomach. "That'll be dinner tonight, for sure."

"Chloe, I don't think this is really—" Professor Ruiz began.

"You'd like one, too? Of course." I beamed and handed him Vietnamese fresh wraps with chili-peanut sauce. Then I hurriedly distributed the rest of the recipes. "Thanks for all the great work, everybody! Oh, looks like class is over. Let me know how the dishes turn out. My e-mail address is on there. I need to hear back from you by Sunday. Just imagine! You'll all have your names in print!" I quickly gathered my belongings and bolted out of the lounge before my professor could protest. My method wasn't the smoothest, most polite way of soliciting recipe testers, but I really had no choice.

I was in an excellent mood during the drive home. Besides having made solid progress on the cookbook, I'd just recruited recipe testers. What's more, I was looking forward to a wonderful restaurant opening tomorrow. And I had a hot new dress to boot. Things were looking up.

FIFTEEN

EARLY on Friday evening, my condo looked as if a tornado had swept through and flung my possessions across every available surface. Well, come to think of it, a tornado *had* struck: the tornado's name was Chloe. The living room was absolutely covered in cookbook material and client notes, my bedroom was thick with yet more paper as well as with clothes, and the bathroom had become a solid mass of beauty products. Although I'd spent an obscene amount of time that afternoon getting ready for the Penthouse opening, I'd been slow to realize that I'd need to wear shoes and nylons. While tossing pretty much the entire contents of my dresser and closet onto the bed and the floor, I'd found a pair of strappy navy heels underneath a box of Christmas gift bags and a non-ripped pair of nylons in the back of my pajama drawer. The shoes needed a bit of polishing with a wet washcloth, but they cleaned up fairly well. I'd pulled my hair into the fanciest updo that I could manage without Adrianna's help, and my makeup was flawless. I repeatedly told myself that my obsession with my appearance had nothing to do with Josh and everything to do with Kyle, but the nothing-to-do-with-Josh mantra didn't seem to be sinking in.

Kyle showed up promptly at seven. When I was dating Josh, I'd spent countless hours either waiting for him to get off work or having him entirely cancel on me because the restaurant "needed" him. He was rarely on time, and his perpetual tardiness had always irked me. Kyle, on the other hand, was here when he said he'd be. Unfortunately, this was one time when I'd have been grateful for an extra fifteen minutes so that I could tidy up the place and finish fussing with my hair.

"Come on in! I'll be right out!" I called from the bathroom as I jabbed another pin into my hair. "I'm so sorry about the mess, but you can see how hard I've been working on the book!"

Kyle's warm laugh echoed down the hall, and I heard the back door shut. "Don't worry, we've got time."

I snarled at my reflection. A damn wisp of hair had fallen out of my updo, and it took me a few minutes to fix it. When I finally emerged from the bathroom, I was appalled to see that I hadn't even left a clear spot where Kyle could sit. He stood formally in my small living room, his hands clasped together as he waited.

"God, this is horrible! I'm so sorry!" I quickly rushed to the couch and gathered up my client notes.

"Are you afraid I'm going to read your diary?" he joked.

"Yeah, right. I'm just horrified about this mess." To have left the confidential notes lying around was really inexcusable. Not that Kyle would be terribly intrigued by the details of my internship, but if I intended to behave professionally, I needed to get in the habit of leaving the notes at work, or at least keeping them zipped in my bag.

"Chloe, you look absolutely stunning." Kyle voice was touchingly sincere. "That dress is perfect for you."

I swear that I felt my cheeks heat up. "Thank you," I said with a smile. "And you, sir, look very dapper yourself." Kyle's goatee was trimmed tonight, and I liked his barbered look even better than his usual cute scruffiness. As I was silently admiring his obviously expensive black suit, it occurred to me that he looked like a male escort I could have found online. Even so, he looked great.

"I'd tip my hat to you if I had one." Kyle winked at me. "Should we go get Adrianna and Owen now?"

"Yes. You know, I think this is the first night out they've had together since Patrick was born. Well, the first without the baby along. Owen found a really sweet girl who lives down the street from them to babysit, so if she works out, maybe they'll be able to go out more. Not that they can afford to very often, but they'd like it." I locked up and followed Kyle to his car. "Of course, I'm always happy to sit for Patrick, but it's good for them to have another option."

Kyle double-parked in front of Ade and Owen's building while I went to get my friends. I rang the bell, waited to be buzzed in, and then made my way up the flight of stairs. I stopped outside their door and cringed. They were having some sort of fight. I sighed and knocked.

Ade whipped the door open. "Hi, Chloe," she said rather seriously. "You look smokin'."

"Um, thank you." I glanced at Adrianna and Owen. Both were dressed beautifully, Ade in a long, soft pink dress, and Owen in a remarkably normal-looking suit. But there was one clear problem: Owen was holding Patrick. Glancing around the living room, I saw no sign of a babysitter. "Uh-oh."

"Yeah." Owen nodded. "Our one babysitter got some sort of *Exorcist*-type stomach bug and apparently puked her guts out an hour ago. Her mother called us and apologized, but it's nobody's fault, obviously. Please tell Adrianna that she has to go tonight. I'm fine with staying home."

"No way, Owen," Adrianna said firmly. "I got to go out to dinner with Chloe the other night, and I got my hair done. You haven't been out at all, hon. I want you to go."

"Absolutely not," Owen said as he moved to the love seat. "Patrick and I are in for the night. Besides, now I can take off these uncomfortable clothes." He smiled broadly at his wife. "Go, go, go! I swear I don't mind."

Ade bit her lip as she looked back and forth between Owen and me. "What do you think, Chloe? Am I a rotten mother for wanting to go to a restaurant opening instead of staying home with my son?"

"Of course not. I think you should do whatever you want to. But one of you is coming with me! And right now, because Kyle is downstairs with the engine running."

Owen shooed us away with his hand. "Off you go, ladies!"

"Oh, all right! Fine, I'll go." I was surprised that Ade didn't stomp her foot. "But you're having a guys' night out soon, Owen, okay?"

"I'll take you up on that, babe. Come give me a kiss, and I'll see you and your sexy dress later."

Ade grinned, rushed over to Owen, and planted a long kiss on his lips.

"Okay, lovebirds, the clock is ticking," I said as they continued to kiss. "Seriously, we have to go!"

"I'm coming," Ade said as she slowly pulled away from Owen. "I'll see you later on tonight." After giving Patrick a quick snuggle, she headed for the door.

"God, you two make me sick," I teased. "Good-bye, Owen!" I practically dragged Ade away from her husband as the two blew kisses back and forth. I somehow managed to get her down to the first floor. "Christ, you two are like rabbits now, huh?"

"Very funny. Hey, is that a new dress and coat? They're gorgeous. But aren't you supposed to be saving your money?"

"These? Oh, I got them on sale," I lied. Yes, I had a wee spending problem, but at least I now had a lucrative job. "Here, hop in the front seat," I said pointing to Kyle's car.

"Thanks." She waved to Kyle and opened the door.

I got in the back and pulled my coat around me. Thank God for fake fur! It was so bitterly cold tonight that I felt justified in my extravagant purchase.

"Where's Owen?" Kyle asked with concern as he pulled the car away from the curb. "Is he sick?"

"No," Ade said as she crossed her long legs. "The baby-sitter is. The truth is that we really can't afford to pay for one anyhow, so it's probably for the best. He'll go out another night."

"That's too bad." Kyle turned up the radio. "Oh, I love this song!"

"Me, too!" Ade squealed.

I endured their enthusiastic, if tuneless, rendition of Aerosmith's "Dream On" and momentarily felt like a child being chauffeured around by embarrassing parents. Fortunately, what came on next was an ear-piercing Mariah Carey song that neither of the front-seat karaoke singers wanted to attempt.

"Tonight is going to be fun, huh, ladies?" Kyle said happily. "I can't wait to see how the food is. And everything inside will be new and decorated perfectly. This'll be a blast!" Kyle pulled up to the valet-parking area in front of a tall building smack-dab in the middle of the financial district.

I had to wonder why Kyle was in such a great mood tonight. With a famous chef for a father, he must have been to tons of restaurant openings; it wasn't as though tonight's outing were a novel experience for him. I, on the other hand, was not a regular at these kinds of events. The last one I'd attended had been at Josh's former restaurant, Simmer.

True to its name, the Penthouse was on the top floor of the building. The three of us rode up in a conspicuously modern elevator with mirrored walls surrounded by neon green lights. During the ride, I did my best not to check and recheck my appearance. When the doors opened, we stepped into a luxurious waiting area with rich brown leather seats

and large potted plants. Although there was plenty of seat-
ing, a good-sized crowd stood there, the most notable member of which was a statuesque woman with a red shawl who
was arguing with the hostess. By craning my neck, I managed to get a clear view of the hostess's face and realized that
she was none other than Georgie, Snacker's girlfriend and
Ellie's best friend. Even though her pale skin was flushed
with irritation, she looked striking. Her hair was especially
lovely, short and blonde, styled off her face in soft curls.

"So what if I didn't RSVP? I'm here now. Can you or can
you not see this fricking invitation in my hand?" The irate
guest waved a paper around wildly. "My best friend is one
of your investors, and believe me, she is going to be furious
if you don't have me and my guests seated in the next five
minutes."

My, my. A quick glance around told me that there were a
number of other diners who had also showed up without re-
plying to the invitation. Kyle caught my eye and snickered
at the crowd around us. He politely nudged his way through
to the hostess and gave Georgie our names, eliciting a sigh
of relief. Georgie caught my eye and waved briefly, beckon-
ing me over. She was probably thrilled to have at least a
few people here who had RSVP'd and could be seated at a
table.

Ade and I followed Kyle and Georgie through the im-
mense dining area. An extraordinary amount of work had
clearly gone into decorating the restaurant: the walls were
a warm champagne color, small drop lights hung from the
ceiling and spotlighted each table, light bamboo floors gave
a feeling of airiness, and more large tropical palms were in

abundance in the main room. The effect was stylish and romantic.

Georgie's attitude did not, however, match the décor. She stomped midway across the room, abruptly stopped at a table for four, slapped the menus down, and exhaled loudly. "Hey, Chloe, sorry about the mob up front. Nobody knows what the hell is going on or where anything is. This is an effing fiasco." She thrust a hand onto her hip and watched as we took our seats. "There aren't enough menus, so you'll have to share. And I'm sorry to tell you that Ellie is going to be your server tonight. Good luck." With that, she turned and marched back to the hostess stand.

Ade scooted her chair in. "Well, isn't she charming? Who was that?"

"That is Georgie, Snacker's girlfriend," I explained. "She certainly looks stressed out."

"No matter," Kyle said cheerfully, shaking his napkin out and setting it formally in his lap. "I'm sure they'll work out the kinks. Oh, it seems I'm missing a fork. And a spoon. Here, Chloe, you take one menu, and I'll share with Adrianna."

"Thanks, Kyle." I smiled and took the menu from his hand.

I alternated between reading the menu and sneaking peeks around the room to see whether Josh was here. Where would he be sitting? There was no sign of him at any of the tables, but his presence was evident on the menu. I glared at the laminated page in my hand. "Vegetable Spring Rolls with Mango Sauce and Sweet Soy." That was Josh's dish. In fact, those spring rolls were one of the first things Josh had ever made for me, and they were goddamn outstanding: thick fried rolls stuffed with tons of shredded vegetables and seasoned with a spice blend that Josh had kept a mystery even from me. I was pissed. And then I saw that another dish, "Clams in a Spicy Orange Bouillon," was also his! I slapped the menu down on my plate.

"Chloe?" Ade looked at me with concern. "Are you okay?"

"Oh, sorry. Everything is fine. Just trying to decide what to order."

I was fuming. It seemed to me that as the executive chef, Snacker should be coming up with his own dishes and not stealing from other chefs. Snacker had done more than learn from Josh; he'd copied Josh's recipes. Snacker was a decent chef, but he was no Josh. Or Digger. I hated to think it, but if Snacker was filching Josh's dishes, just how ambitious was he? Maybe more than I'd thought. Maybe he'd been willing to do whatever it took to get Digger's job.

Sixteen

"GOOD evening. Can I take your drink orders? Oh, Chloe! Hi." Ellie stood by our table.

"Ellie, it's good to see you," I said tentatively. I hadn't forgotten that she was capable of launching into four-letter-word tirades with no notice.

"Wonderful!" She beamed too broadly and flipped her full head of hair to the side. She'd clearly just reapplied her bright lipstick. I couldn't help staring at the thick paste on her lips. "I'm glad you could make it. So, would you like some wine to start with while you go over the menu?"

"Actually, I'm ready to order," Kyle said. "Are you ladies ready, too?"

Adrianna nodded, and I shrugged. "Sure," I said. My

mood was going downhill by the minute. At the moment, I didn't particularly care about the food. "Why don't you start?"

"We seem to be missing some silverware," said Kyle, pointing to the table. "When you have a chance, maybe we could get some more?"

"Absolutely!" Ellie said enthusiastically.

I paid almost no attention to what my dinner companions ordered or even to my own choices. I watched Ellie as she walked away. She seemed to be trying too hard tonight. Her chipper attitude struck me as a front. Adrianna and Kyle were too engaged in nonstop conversation with each other to notice either Ellie's hyped-up state or my own odd mood. Although I was happy that Ade was enjoying her rare night out, I was so distracted by hoping for—or dreading?—a Josh sighting that I limited myself to meaningless nods and smiles.

Our appetizers arrived and proved to be mediocre at best, or so I thought. When Kyle declared the cold potato cakes delightful, I refrained from pointing out that they were supposed to be hot; I was once again less than impressed with the cookbook writer's palate. With a knowing look, Adrianna gave me a taste of her tuna carpaccio with wasabi cream, a dish that should have been really hard to screw up but was somehow flavorless. My Mediterranean shrimp were not tremendously Mediterranean, but they were edible.

"How's the shrimp, Chloe? Should we try for this recipe for the book?" Kyle lifted his eyebrows in question.

"Um, maybe. Let's see what else we try tonight, and then we can decide," I said. Ade and Kyle seemed to be having such a good time that I avoided pointing out obvious flaws. Besides, I was still wondering where Josh was. I had on this damn dress, and I intended to have him see me in it! He just had to be here, if not at a table, maybe at the bar? In the kitchen? Having run out of patience, I excused myself to go to the ladies' room. Ladies' room trip or covert spy mission to locate a hot ex—same thing, right?

A supposed search for the ladies' room gave me a good excuse to wander around. A thorough search for Josh in the main dining room and the separate bar area toward the front of the restaurant yielded no cute chefs. I strolled casually to the back of the dining room and ended up near the kitchen. I obviously couldn't just barge in there, but maybe I could snag a glance inside when a server opened the door.

"Chloe, can I help you with something?" Ellie stopped me and gave me a suspicious look.

"Oh, Ellie. Ahem. I was trying to find the ladies' room."

"It is sort of hidden. Right there." She pointed to a cluster of the leafy palms that sat in elaborate ceramic planters near the kitchen entrance. In front of the plants was a mobile service station with extra dishes, glasses, napkins, and silverware. "The owners didn't want a glaring sign for the bathroom, so they created a plant wall to disguise the area."

"Thanks." I smiled and made my way around the plants and into the luxurious ladies' room. The front section was set up as a plush lounge area. Three white vanity tables had matching stools with cushions. Samples of body lotions, soaps, and hair sprays nestled in small baskets, and soft hand towels were stacked in perfect piles on a narrow table. I sank into a flowered armchair and waited a few minutes. I was feeling much more comfortable in here than I'd been while skulking around the restaurant. Curiosity soon got the best of me, though. I left the bathroom only to walk straight into one of the large palm leaves that dangled across my path.

"Stupid plant," I muttered, swatting the leaf away. I took a step and then froze as I heard Josh's voice coming from nearby, presumably from the service station. Still hidden behind the palm, I leaned in. He was speaking so softly that I could barely make out what he was saying.

". . . really hot . . . more than Snacker can handle . . ."

I thrust my head into the foliage and frowned. Peering past the greenery, I saw that Josh was whispering into Georgie's ear. Stupid, willowy blonde with magnificent hair! She was "really hot," of course. But was she more than Snacker could handle? But not more than my Josh could handle? Could Georgie be the real reason that Josh had come back to Boston? I winced as he brushed her hair back and continued whispering. God, he was messing around with Snacker's girlfriend! He and Snacker were friends. They'd worked together, they were former roommates, and Josh was temporarily staying with Snacker at their old apartment—where Georgie undoubtedly spent plenty of time, too.

This new and unwelcome knowledge about Josh was what I deserved for spying on people. I pulled away. I wanted nothing more than to flee, to go home, and never to have to see Josh in the vicinity of another woman again. I felt sick. And here I was stuck behind these plants! What was up with all these palms? It's not like this was Florida! My leg bounced nervously, and I opened and closed my hands repeatedly as I tried to figure out how to escape without running into anyone. Failing to come up with an imaginative plan, I settled for tucking my head down and making a break for it. Simple was best, I decided. I'd just walk straight back to the table and behave normally.

Having started to do exactly that, I got about six feet before I crashed into Josh.

"Whoa, Chloe. Slow down." Josh put his hands on my arms, forcing me to stop.

I looked up at him slowly, taking in his white chef's coat and bright blue eyes. That damn tan was still there, too. Bastard. "Hello, Josh. Excuse me." I made a move to leave, but he held me in place.

"How . . . how are you?" he asked gently.

"Fine. I'm here with a date. I should go." I cast my eyes down and refused to look at him.

"You take Adrianna along on all your dates?" he asked. "Or only on the ones with assholes like that?"

"What?" I met his eyes now. "Kyle and I are writing a book together." Fine, it was a bit of an exaggeration. "We invited Adrianna and Owen to come out with us tonight. Owen had to stay at home with Patrick. But the point is, I'm getting on with my life."

"Chloe, you don't know the first thing about that guy. Hey, wait!" He tried to stop me, but I pulled away. "You've got to hear about . . . Please talk to me, Chloe," he begged as I stormed off.

I returned to my table, where Adrianna and Kyle were deep in conversation and didn't appear to have noticed my absence. Our entrées had arrived. I started to pick at my pork with Gorgonzola risotto. It could have been cat food and I wouldn't have noticed.

"Owen would love to have another baby right away, but I'm mixed about it," Adrianna was saying. "I wouldn't mind getting the whole diaper business over with as soon as possible, while Patrick is still a baby, but it just seems like so much work, you know? And we really can't afford to have another kid right now, anyhow."

"But you'd like to have more?" Kyle rested his arms on the table.

"Sure, I'd love to someday, but probably not right now. Owen loves, loves, loves being a father, and he can be really insistent when he gets his mind set on something." She shrugged. "We'll see who wins this argument."

"I didn't know you were talking about having more babies," I said, perking up. "You guys seem to make great kids, so I'm all for it. Besides, you already have all the baby gear you'll need."

Adrianna rolled her eyes. "Yeah, well, you can talk to Owen about waking his ass up to feed the next one, because so far I'm the only food machine in the house. Oh my God, Chloe, you have to taste this beef tenderloin."

Ade stuck a forkful of perfectly cooked beef at me. Okay, this dish was outstanding. The cream and horseradish sauce went perfectly with the pepper-encrusted beef. Somebody in the kitchen was doing something right, even though most of the food was disappointing.

After our plates had been cleared, Georgie appeared at our table. "Would you all like dessert tonight?" she asked.

I stared at my wineglass, unable even to look at the tramp!

God, how dare she ask if I'd like dessert while she was fooling around with Josh! I wanted to stand up and slap the girl, shout that she wasn't allowed near my Josh, that I hated her. I exerted self-control, refusing to make a tableside spectacle of myself. "Excuse me." I hurriedly got up from my chair and rushed back toward the ladies' room. Once again hovering behind the potted palms outside the entrance, I parted the leaves, peered through, watched my table, and waited until Georgie had left.

At first, Georgie seemed to be heading directly toward me, but her actual destination was the serving station, where she began fussing with plates and silverware. I figured I'd be able to slip past the potted palm and scoot back to the table without running into her, but just as I began to move, Ellie and her lipsticked mouth showed up, and she began berating her supposed friend.

"You're such a bitch, do you know that?" Ellie was making no effort to keep her voice down.

Georgie ran a finger over a perfectly waxed eyebrow and stared pointedly at Ellie. "People who read other people's e-mail have only themselves to blame if they don't like what they find out. Excuse me. I have guests to attend to."

Whoa, this was getting interesting.

"Hey, missy!" Ellie blocked Georgie's path. "I only read Digger's e-mail after he was dead. I wanted to get in touch with people who cared about him and let them know what had happened to him," she seethed.

"Yeah, right!" Georgie scoffed. "You were probably reading his e-mail and scanning his text messages even before he died. I bet you've been sneaky all along, and you killed

Digger yourself out of jealousy! You should've known what chefs are like, dummy."

"Well, I know what you're like. You're a slut, Georgie. A total slut!"

"Hey, watch your mouth. I am a very loving and caring person."

Ellie crossed her arms and glared at her ex-friend. "Loving person? You have some nerve describing yourself like that after what you've done. Murderous person is more like it!"

"What?"

"Yeah, I'm starting to think that you're the one who killed Digger. You were probably hoping that by getting him out of the way, Snacker would get this chef job. Well, congratulations, you stupid bitch! You did it! Happy now?"

"Okay, little Miss Self-Righteous, listen here—"

Before Georgie had time to sling her next insult, a neatly dressed man with a pale purple tie stepped firmly between the two girls. He looked beyond furious but managed a threatening whisper behind a false smile. "Not one more word out of either of you. If we weren't hopelessly understaffed right now, I'd fire you on the spot! This sort of scene is totally inexcusable. Get back to work immediately!"

Georgie and Ellie both hurried off, appropriately chagrined.

Well, well! So not only was perfect, skinny Georgie doing whatever she was doing with Josh and Snacker, but she'd been fooling around with Digger, too! I usually didn't mind a little juicy gossip, but I felt sorry for Ellie, who had seemed so committed to her chef. She'd been driven in her determination to help him succeed professionally, and when I'd broken the news of Digger's death, she'd gone to pieces. But this new information did explain her sudden change in demeanor on the phone the other day. One possibility was that she'd taken Digger's computer from his apartment and found out about the affair only when she'd read his e-mail. Or, I reasoned, Georgie could be right that Ellie had in fact known about the relationship earlier and had taken the computer to destroy the evidence of her possible motive. Could either of these young women really have killed Digger? I shuddered.

I left the all-too-familiar potted-plant area and returned to the table. My prolonged absence had again gone so totally unnoticed that I was beginning to develop a third-wheel complex. Adrianna and Kyle, who were discussing the writer's relationship with his father, barely acknowledged me when I sat down.

"Look, Kyle," Ade was saying, "your father is a very accomplished and, frankly, awe-inspiring person, so it's no wonder you feel such pressure to succeed. But this cookbook sounds like it's coming along wonderfully, and you're bound to impress him with how hard you've worked. You need to look at your accomplishments for what they are, though. Yours. Take pride in what you've done."

Kyle grinned sheepishly. "I guess you're right. I've put my heart and soul into this book. And I'll admit that I think I've really got a knack for this kind of project."

I refrained from laughing. The truth was that I was the one who had been doing all of the work on this goddamn book! God, what a crap night.

"Exactly." Adrianna nodded and then touched his arm. "Kyle, even if your father can't see how talented you are, you can still feel good about yourself."

As I watched Adrianna put her hand on Kyle, I had to remind myself that she was deeply committed to Owen and that I was seeing nothing more than harmless flirting. In fact, now that I looked at her again, I realized that she really wasn't flirting at all; rather, she was being motherly. *Awww!* This new side to Adrianna was one that I really loved. Up until the minute Patrick was born, Adrianna had been the least maternal person I'd ever met. But things had changed.

"Oh, good. Dessert!" Ade sat up tall in her chair to get a glimpse of the plates that Georgie was bringing our way.

"I can't wait to taste that layered chocolate thing I ordered. What was it called, Ade?" Kyle asked.

"I don't remember, but it did sound good."

"You'll have to try some."

Georgie silently distributed desserts. I held absolutely still as she placed my plate in front of me, lest I involuntarily reach up and scratch her eyes out. When Kyle ordered coffee for the table, Georgie gave a perfunctory nod.

"Chloe, I ordered you a dessert, too," Kyle said. "Pumpkin cheesecake tarts. Is that okay?"

"Thank you. That sounds delicious." The three small cheesecakes on my plate had gingersnap crusts and were garnished with melted chocolate. One bite of the pumpkin delights took the edge off my depressed spirit.

Although Ade and Kyle traded bites of his chocolate dish and her chestnut-and-banana-bread pudding, no one asked for a taste of my yummy pumpkin tarts. I wasn't exactly jealous, but I wasn't thrilled.

Kyle excused himself to go to the men's room.

"The guest-of-honor table, I see!" Snacker surprised me from behind by clapping his hands down onto my shoulders.

"Snacker!" It was so good to see him. Although I'd missed Snacker, he was one of the people I'd lost touch with after Josh and I had broken up; it hadn't felt right to call Josh's best friend on my own. So, despite tonight's crummy events, I was glad I'd come just for the chance to see Snacker. His white chef's coat acted as a foil for his olive skin and dark curly hair. He'd obviously put on a clean coat to make his rounds in the dining room; this coat had no stains at all. He was doing his best to hide his fatigue and stress behind a broad grin and an air of high energy.

"It's so nice to see you," I said honestly as I stood and gave him a big hug. "Congratulations."

He squeezed me tightly and lifted me off my feet. "Hello, Adrianna," he said politely. Snacker and Adrianna maintained a cordial relationship for my sake, but because of their ill-timed smooch sessions, each tried to stay out of the other's way.

"Hello, Snacker," Ade said with as much warmth as she could muster.

Snacker lowered me to the floor, put his hands on his hips, and checked out our desserts. "How was everything? I know we've still got some kinks to work out."

"Everything was outstanding," I said. It wasn't true, of course, but I'd never have told Snacker about the snags in the service or the wavering quality of the food.

"Christ, I hardly had any notice about coming on as the executive chef. Damn shame about Digger. I still can't believe it. I probably wouldn't even have taken the job, but my girlfriend really wanted me to accept. Have you met Georgie?"

I nodded. "Um, yes. She seems . . . very . . . very nice." If by *very nice* I meant that she was sleeping with most of the city.

"Yeah, well, she wants us to move in together, and I need the money, so I went ahead and took the job. Thank God for Josh, though. Tonight would've been a royal disaster if he hadn't stepped in and helped out in the kitchen."

"You'd never know there'd been problems. Honestly, it was a great meal," Ade said.

"I hate to run, but I'm supposed to walk around the dining room and schmooze everyone." Snacker leaned down to give me another hug and whispered in my ear. "Chloe, have you and Josh talked?"

I nodded weakly. "Sort of. There's no point."

"Yes, there is. Don't give up yet." He squeezed my arm and then left to finish his executive-chef table duties.

"Chloe? Are you okay?" Ade asked, concerned.

I shrugged. "I guess so." I quickly filled her in on what I'd seen and overheard.

Ade's jaw dropped open. "Josh and Georgie?"

"It seems so," I said morosely.

"And Digger and Georgie."

"It seems so, too."

"God, what a whore."

"That's about what Ellie said."

"Good for her. She should be pissed!"

"Maybe she was too pissed. Maybe Ellie offed her boyfriend for cheating on her with her best friend. Or maybe Georgie killed Digger to get Snacker the job. She got close to Digger so she could talk him out of the job or have access to his house and burn it down."

"Good God. What the hell is going on with everybody? It seems like everyone is going crazy."

"I know," I said, now halfheartedly eating my dessert. "At the rate things are going, I could be next."

SEVENTEEN

SATURDAY morning found me nursing a restaurant-opening hangover, not from alcohol, but from emotional overload. To avoid dealing with anything that had happened the previous night, I pumped myself full of coffee and got deliberately lost in the cookbook. It was much easier to focus on page-number styles, recipe formats, and chapter titles than on Josh's fling with Georgie. I plowed through my notes, wrote speedily, and by mid-afternoon had e-mailed Kyle an outline of the book, a draft of the chapter about appetizers, and a handful of recipes. I recorded the number of hours I'd worked and submitted those, too.

I took a long steaming-hot bath and distractedly pumiced my feet so overzealously that I doubted whether I'd be able to walk comfortably for a week; I had removed most of the skin from the soles and heels. I was a wrinkled prune when I finally I got out, wrapped myself in a thick robe, and put on heavy socks. Kyle called as I was running a comb through my knotted hair.

"I just read through everything you sent, Chloe, and it's fabulous. Really good work," he complimented me.

"Thank you," I said, pleased that he could see how hard I had worked.

"Did you have a good time last night?"

"Yes," I lied. "Restaurant openings are always so intense. You can feel the energy in the air."

"I thought that the food was fantastic and the company even better."

"You and Adrianna get along well, huh?"

"She's obviously a good friend. I can see why you two are so close. It was helpful to talk to her about my father. She really seemed to get how demanding he is."

So much for the thousands of dollars being spent on my social work degree! Maybe I just needed to have a baby, and then I'd magically become a better listener. But truthfully, I was glad that Kyle appreciated Adrianna. Typically, women envied her looks and didn't see beyond her beauty, and men were so dazzled by her appearance that they couldn't see her as a friend.

"Anyway," Kyle continued, "my father is here again, and he'd like to go over what there is of the book so far, mostly so that he can write his introduction. You know, 'I'm Hank Boucher, famous chef, everyone loves me, blah, blah, blah.'

I'll give him what I have so far. That should be enough to get him going."

While I understood that the effort I was putting into the cookbook was simply considered "work for hire," it was increasingly clear to me that I was the only one actually writing anything! Yes, work for hire meant that I was paid for my time and owned no legal rights to the book. Still, if the Boucher boys wanted to be fair, they might consider giving me coauthor status. Kyle, however, probably had no power to make decisions about the book; I'd have to go straight to the top.

"Kyle, I have a thought," I said casually. "Why don't you bring your father by for dinner tomorrow evening? I can make some of the dishes from the book. I'd love to spend some time with him. Maybe it would help to give me a better feel for the book as a whole."

"Chloe, I really don't want to subject you to an entire evening with my father. Besides, you don't want to cook for the man. Trust me."

The more I thought about the possibility of being a coauthor, the more determined I was to lure Chef Boucher to my condo. "We'll compromise. How about just appetizers and drinks? I'll have everything ready when you get here. It'll just be a quick pop-in visit."

Kyle paused. "Okay. If you insist."

"Besides, he should taste what's going to be in the book, don't you think?"

"You're probably right. But don't say I didn't warn you. He's picky. He'll tear apart anything he doesn't love, so I hope you're thick-skinned."

"I'll wear a suit of armor," I said. "Don't worry about anything."

I hung up and began making a shopping list. I was happy to keep busy, and busy I'd be: preparing appetizers for Hank Boucher would be a challenge, but if I wanted a shot at co-authorship, I'd better not screw up.

When the list was done, I called Adrianna in the hope of finding yet another way to occupy myself, but she didn't pick up, and I figured she might be squeezing in a nap. I hopped online and tried to waste some time. Perez Hilton's gossip blog featured shots of Daniel Craig emerging from the ocean, Miley Cyrus giving her usual stupid peace sign, and Brad Pitt surrounded by his eight million children. I clicked on my bookmarks and went to the Desperate Chefs' Wives blog. I loved the site, which I'd visited regularly until Josh had ditched me for the Hawaii sun. The young woman who ran the blog was married to a chef and posted all sorts of funny stories about life with him. She wrote about watching *Top Chef* with her husband, she complained about how crummy his schedule was, she posted restaurant reviews, and she dropped lots of general tidbits about life with a chef. I especially enjoyed the blogs that she titled Chef Mumbles, which were about her husband's habit of talking in his sleep. Even when he was zonked out, his mind stayed on his work: "It's for the tasting menu. For Neil Patrick Harris," he'd say in his sleep, and "I need dill and salsify." He liked to engage his sleeping wife in conversation, too. "Is your station ready?" he once asked, to which his awakened wife begrudgingly replied that, yes, it was. "No. It's not," the chef responded before retreating back into silent sleep. In addition to mumbling, her husband sometimes hopped out of bed in the middle of the night, put on his chef pants, got back under the covers, and slept for another three hours.

I missed all of it. Josh, too, used to talk in his sleep, rattling off lists of ingredients or details about scheduling. I knew that I should stop reading the blog, but I couldn't help myself. The familiarity somehow made me feel close to Josh.

I checked another blog that I was nuts about, Chef's Widow, where the CW (as she refers to herself and to other women involved with rarely seen chefs) chronicles life with her chef and their two children. She'd posted great videos of her kids and pictures of her few-and-far-between dates with her husband, and she wrote honest, raw, sometimes painful accounts of her life. Her whole world felt so recognizable, so much like mine—minus the cute kids—that I momentarily cheered up. Then I checked my cell phone, saw three missed calls from Josh, refused to listen to the messages, and deleted all three. Crap.

I slept miserably that night and must have done some mumbling of my own. I had powerful, horrible dreams about Josh, Digger, and Snacker, the kinds of blurry dreams that you can't remember in detail but that sure as hell leave you with an awful, gut-wrenching feeling when you wake up. I hauled myself out of bed and tried to shower off the bad night's sleep, but it took a few cups of coffee to shake off the residue of my nightmares. I always hated Sunday anyway, because it meant school and work were imminent. Still, I had to rouse myself: Hank and Kyle were coming for appetizers and drinks at five o'clock. Because I had a lot to do,

I went out and did the food shopping early. I'd need plenty of time to prep the food and clean the house, which was even more of a mess than it had been on Friday when I'd left for the opening of the Penthouse.

I was tackling a few seafood appetizers tonight: seared scallops served on polenta cakes with red pepper and chive jam, and also baked oysters with heavy cream, turmeric, fennel, and Asian pear. But the one I was most eager to eat myself was the shrimp and Brie wrapped in puff pastry and served with apricot chutney. Any excuse to eat melted Brie, and I was all over it! I'd bought a very expensive bottle of dry Riesling and an equally pricey bottle of Viognier that had a subtle floral note. I put on the stereo and listened to music while I pureed red peppers. I added sugar to the peppers and cooked the mixture down to a thick consistency before I added chives. I whisked the polenta in a pot and then spread it out on a sheet pan to let it set before I cut out circles to panfry. I chopped the fresh apricots and cooked them with water, honey, vinegar, and onions until I had a chunky sweet-and-sour chutney. I then cut the store-bought phyllo dough and made little purses that I filled with shrimp and Brie and then brushed with an egg wash. At best, I'd have Hank Boucher's attention for a very short time, so I wanted to have as much prep as possible completed before he arrived; otherwise, I'd waste my opportunity by disappearing into the kitchen.

Since I was trying to impress upon Hank that I was worthy of being a coauthor, I intended to look professional. Consequently, I put on a pair of straight-leg dress pants and a pale green linen shirt. My condo was white-glove clean, and candles burned in the living room. Wineglasses and the two bottles of wine were ready on the coffee table, and I'd set out small hand-painted ceramic plates as well as forks and carefully ironed cloth napkins. *Whew!* I was as prepared for the celebrity chef's visit as I could be.

To my surprise, Kyle and Hank arrived precisely at five o'clock; I'd expected Kyle's busy father to cause some sort of delay. When I opened my door, one look at Kyle's face told me how stressed he was about this evening. I smiled reassuringly at Kyle as I said hello

"Hi, Chloe." Kyle's voice shook.

"Good evening, Chloe. It's a pleasure to see you again," said Hank with no hint of sincerity. "We can't stay too long. We have dinner reservations later this evening."

"Of course. I understand. Please come in and sit down." I pointed to the couch as I took their coats.

Hank dumped himself onto the couch and sighed. "I hear you're attempting to cook something for us? Something from the book?"

Attempting? What a jerk. "Yes. Appetizers. I just need a few minutes to finish them off. Can I pour you a glass of wine?"

Hank inspected the two bottles and raised his eyebrows, as if he were as amazed by my choices as he was pleased with them. "This one." He tapped the Riesling, sat back against the cushion, and checked his watch.

"Kyle?" I asked as I poured Hank's wine. He nodded, and since he looked in need of alcohol, I filled his glass high. "Give me ten minutes, and the appetizers will be ready."

I walked quickly to the kitchen and was glad that I'd

had the foresight to preheat the oven and to set out all the pans that I'd need. I stuck the sheet of phyllo purses and the tray of oysters into the oven. While they cooked, I quickly seared the scallops and the polenta cakes in a pan and hastily plated everything on serving trays. Well, I told myself, my presentation wasn't as stupendous as a professional chef's, but it wasn't awful, either. I carried two of the trays to the living room. "Kyle, would you mind getting the other tray and the two small bowls with sauces?"

"Of course." Kyle practically jumped out of his seat at the opportunity to escape his father. I wondered why he was so fearful of his father. Granted, Hank struck me as a pig, but I had the sense something else was going on, something new, maybe, or an exacerbation of something old, but I didn't know what it was.

Kyle seemed to take forever in the kitchen. Although in most circumstances I'm more than capable of small talk, I felt intimidated, and Hank said nothing at all; the two of us waited in silence for Kyle to return. When he finally did, I glared at him in annoyance.

"All right, let's see what you have here, Chloe." Hank peered skeptically at my appetizers.

I succinctly described each dish and then poured myself a hefty glass of wine; if the food didn't go over well, I could always get drunk and wash away the memory.

Hank helped himself to an oyster. When I'd put a few appetizers on my own plate, I watched nervously as he lifted the shell and slid the oyster into his mouth. Now I knew how those poor Iron Chefs felt waiting for the judges' decisions!

"Outstanding," Hank proclaimed. "The turmeric and

cream are spot on with the fennel and pear." He nodded thoughtfully. "And perfectly cooked. Nothing worse than an overcooked oyster, for God's sake."

As Kyle beamed at me, the muscles in his face relaxed a bit. "How about this scallop, Dad? Want to try that next?" Kyle took a gulp of wine and then sampled the scallop. "What did you say this was, Chloe? Red pepper jam? It's very nice."

I froze mid-bite and silently willed Kyle to shut up. Didn't he understand that as the presumed writer of the cookbook, he should know exactly what the dishes were and precisely what ingredients they contained? How could he fail to realize that, in asking me questions, he was giving himself away?

"Wow! And that little doughy thing looks nice," he continued. "Cheese and shrimp, right?"

When Hank caught my eye, I knew that the inevitable would happen, and I quickly looked away. Oblivious, Kyle rambled on about how delightful the appetizers were and how sure he was that his father's book would be a best seller.

I drank more wine. "Yes, I think the book will do very well," I agreed, trying to keep the conversation moving while depriving Hank of the opportunity to speak. "We still have some blanks to fill in, but I know that you have a number of chef and restaurant leads, right, Kyle?"

"Oh, yes. Dad, I haven't had a chance to tell you about some of the most recent contacts I've made, have I?"

Hank was finishing a scallop. He set his fork and napkin down. "No, Kyle, you haven't. But there is something else that concerns me more." He looked pointedly at his son. I winced. We hadn't fooled Hank. "You don't recognize these appetizers, do you? They aren't the least bit familiar to you."

Kyle coughed and set his plate down. "What? Um . . . what do you . . . ?" he stammered.

Hank stood up, marched across the living room, and came to a halt, his back toward Kyle. "I should have known. You stupid, incompetent, lazy ass!" The chef spun around. His face was red and his eyes full of anger. "These are from the cookbook, moron!" he shouted. "The book that you are supposedly writing! Remember that one?"

I hung my head in embarrassment for Kyle, who obviously hadn't even glanced at the recipes or the chapter that I'd sent him. I couldn't look at either of the men.

"No, Dad, that's not true," Kyle started. "I just forgot. I didn't recognize them at first. I mean, there are so many dishes in the cookbook and—"

"Shut up! Shut your mouth!" Hank barked. "I should have known. Really. I shouldn't have expected you to do a goddamn thing! Chloe here did all of the work while you did shit. She is the writer, not you. I might as well just rip your name off of this project and hand the whole book over to someone who is actually willing to lift a finger and do something with her life!"

Okay, yes, I'd wanted to worm my way into becoming an official coauthor, but my plan had spun out of control. Kyle had no excuse for having failed even to read what he was supposed to have written, but he certainly didn't deserve this humiliating excoriation.

"No, Mr. Boucher, really!" I protested, willing to forgo my shot at being a coauthor. "I'm just a research assistant. Kyle has collected so much information, including most of the recipes, and he's made a lot of chef contacts. I've just put everything together."

Hank glared at me. "Nice try, but I'm not buying it. God, Kyle, after all the opportunities I've given you? You've had your miserable life handed to you on a platter, and yet you somehow manage to screw up even the most menial job! Do you think I got where I am today by acting like a tool? Do you think that beautiful women will get within ten feet of a cheat like you? God, no wonder you've never been married," Hank screamed, laughing viciously. "I try and I try and I just get nowhere with you. I'm disgusted!"

As the chef continued his onslaught, I tried to block out the barrage of insults. The painful scene pointedly reminded me of my client Danny and his abusive, controlling, condescending father. I thought about my classmate's comment that Danny's father had spent so many years foretelling his son's failure that his predictions had become self-fulfilling prophecies. In Hank Boucher's eyes, Kyle had failed over and over. I suspected that he'd left me stuck with most of the cookbook work not because he was lazy, but because he assumed that nothing he produced would satisfy his demanding father.

"And if you think for one minute that I'm buying this crap about your intense involvement in this book, then you better think again. Idiot!"

"Dad, I'm sorry," Kyle pleaded pathetically. "Let's just leave." He started to look at me and then quickly turned away.

"Yes, of course we're leaving, dumbass!" Hank shook his head at his son and then walked slowly over to me. Suddenly his voice was soft and calm. "Chloe Carter, you have done remarkable work. You should be proud of yourself. The chapter I read was outstanding. Crisp, clear, engaging. The recipes were formatted precisely, and the directions were easy to follow. Good work." He stuck his hand out, and I had no choice but to shake it. The monster! I was too flabbergasted and too sorry for Kyle even to mutter perfunctory thanks.

I silently retrieved Kyle's and Hank's coats, and then opened the door. Hank held his head high as he walked out and continued to lavish unwanted praise on me. "Fabulous, my dear. Nicely done! I'll be in touch."

I touched Kyle's arm as he left. He turned his head slightly my way. "I'm so, so sorry."

"It'll be fine. This will blow over, and we'll keep working on the cookbook. You'll see," I tried to reassure him.

"No. You don't get it. It's over for me. I just . . . I'm sorry." He rushed out the door to catch up with his father.

I looked at my coffee table, still covered in serving dishes that held the food that I'd slaved over. What moments ago had been a gorgeous display of culinary delights now looked hopelessly sad to me; I had never intended to have my cooking and my work used against Kyle. I helped myself to an oyster and pondered Hank's outburst. As a budding social worker, I knew that Hank's behavior must be rooted in his own past. He'd probably grown up in a terrible family and was now passing on his pain to his son. Still! I just couldn't understand how any father could treat his son that way, especially in front of someone else. Granted, Hank had given Kyle the chance to write the cookbook, but he seemed to have done so mainly to create an opportunity to belittle his son. Of course, Kyle was rather incompetent, but how the hell was anyone expected to succeed under Hank Boucher's cruel guidance? That demeaning, abusive, hateful scene was tantamount to emotional murder.

Murder. It occurred to me that Hank was in Boston when Digger died. Kyle and Hank were supposed to meet me at Digger's that morning. When they'd arrived in the rented Hummer, Hank had been driving, so he'd obviously had Digger's address, and might have had it the previous evening or in the early morning. And Hank was certainly a horrible person, maybe horrible enough to commit murder. Look how he had exploded at Kyle! And right in front of me. I hated to imagine how his temper flared when there were no witnesses. But what possible motive could he have had for killing Digger? As far as I knew, Hank had never even met Digger.

I nibbled on shrimp-and-Brie puffs and gave silent thanks for having parents who loved me, who wanted the best for me, and who would never, ever subject me to public humiliation.

EIGHTEEN

ON Thursday, four days after the appetizer disaster, I still hadn't heard from Kyle or Hank. I couldn't bear to call Kyle, who was probably licking his wounds and would get in touch with me once they'd begun to heal. In spite of my sympathy for him, I couldn't help being curious about the status of the cookbook. I needed the job as much as ever and needed to know whether Hank had scrapped the project or whether we were still writing the book.

I was coming home from my supervision group when I noticed Owen's obtrusive fish truck parked by the sidewalk in front of my house. Maneuvering my car into my spot, I eyed the seafood company's logo on the side of the truck: WE'LL GIVE YOU CRABS. *God!* No wonder Owen's business was doing badly. I could see Owen in his side mirror. He was bouncing his head to music and hadn't noticed my arrival. I snuck up to the driver's side window and startled Owen by pounding on the glass. He jumped. "We don't want any!" I said loudly. "Get your smelly truck outta here!"

Owen laughed and rolled down the window. "You scared the crap out of me, Chloe."

"That was the point. You waiting for me?"

"Yeah. I need to talk to you."

"Do you want to come up?"

"Nah, I can't stay too long. How 'bout you hop in? It's nice and warm, and I've got AM radio," he said in a sing-song voice.

"In that case, sure. You know how I love AM radio. When else can I hear Paul Anka?" I rolled my eyes but climbed into the passenger's seat. "What's up? Is something going on with Adrianna? Or Patrick?" I wrinkled my nose at the stench. I love seafood, but the smell in the truck was a bit much, even for me. The dolphin air freshener did little to camouflage the fishy reek.

"Nah, Ade and Patrick are fine. Look, Chloe," Owen said, running his hands through his dark hair, "I came to talk to you about Josh."

"No you don't!" I reached for the door handle, but Owen hit the automatic lock button. "Are you seriously keeping me hostage?"

"Yes. Just hear me out."

I crossed my arms and sulked. "Fine. What is it?"

"He really wants to talk to you, and he says that you

won't take his calls and that you brushed him off at the Penthouse's opening."

"Why would I want to talk to him, Owen? He's part of my past, and I'm trying really hard to move on, but no one will let me!" I held back tears.

"First of all, he's really worried about this Kyle that you're working for. He says this guy is a total jerk."

"Yeah, what the hell is his problem with Kyle, anyway? He certainly can't be jealous! Besides, I don't care what Josh thinks."

"Maybe this is just an excuse for Josh to be in touch with you, but he wanted me to tell you that he and Digger went to culinary school with Kyle, so he knows more about Kyle than you think."

What? Kyle had never once mentioned that he'd gone to culinary school. Yes, he'd said that he'd gone to school briefly in Boston, but he certainly hadn't said a thing about culinary school, and he hadn't told me that he'd known Digger. I couldn't remember whether I'd mentioned Josh's last name when we'd discussed Simmer, but Digger was another matter entirely. There weren't all that many Diggers in the world to begin with, and a guy named Digger who was a Boston chef? I was willing to bet that there'd been only one, and I couldn't believe that Kyle had failed to reveal his connection. Furthermore, as I'd learned on the night when I'd cooked with Ade, Owen, and Kyle, the famous chef's son couldn't even cook! As for his taste buds, practically every dish we'd tried during our restaurant outings had tasted good to him; even when food was mediocre or downright awful, he thought that it was just fine. "Oh. Well, I didn't know that Kyle had gone to school with Josh. And so what if Josh doesn't like Kyle? Big deal."

"He misses you, Chloe. Josh really misses you."

"No." I shook my head and looked straight ahead. "No, he doesn't. He's fooling around with Snacker's girlfriend, Georgie. I saw them together the other night." I sniffed and forced a smile. "So how are you doing? What's been going on at your house?"

"Smooth change of subject there," Owen said. "But I'll let it go for now. The truth is that things are sort of tough. The fish business blows, and I promised Adrianna that I'd look online for another job. In fact, that's where I'm headed now. There just has to be something more reliable than this. I really thought that I could make this work, you know? I thought that by now I'd have a bunch of regular restaurants that would give me all of their business and that I'd be making fat commissions off all of them." He shrugged and looked solemn and disturbingly un-Owen-like.

"I'm sure you'll find something soon. Who wouldn't want to hire you? You've got tons of experience in so many areas," I said, trying to put a positive spin on Owen's erratic work history.

"We'll see. Adrianna and Patrick are going to be gone for a while tonight, so I'll really be able to concentrate on this job search. It's hard to pay attention when my beautiful wife and entertaining son are around."

"Where is Ade going? I could watch Patrick for you guys if you need me," I offered.

"Thanks, but she's going to a clothing swap set up by her

online mothers' group. I guess they're meeting at one of the mom's houses for a potluck. Ade has a big bag of clothes that Patrick has already outgrown, but mostly I think she's getting out of the house to make me stick to my job hunt. She knows me too well." He laughed and then turned serious again. "I feel like I'm letting her down."

I leaned over and gave Owen a hug. "She adores you, Owen, and you could never let her down. Never."

"Thanks, Chloe. I love her, too."

"I know you do." I kissed Owen on the cheek and stepped out of the truck. "You better get off to that job search, mister."

"Hey," he started, "please think about talking to Josh. I think you're blowing things here. He is still in love with you, Chloe."

"Tough!" I shut the door.

"And you're in love with him!" Owen called out the window as I walked away. "You know you are!"

"Shut up, Owen!" I laughed over my shoulder. He meant well, but he wasn't doing much to bolster the supposedly independent–woman theme I had going.

I was wiped out. When I reached my condo, I immediately yanked off my mental-health-professional clothes and pulled on cozy sweatpants and thick socks. I was going to hunker down in front of Thursday-night television and work my way through a carton of ice cream. I rooted through my dresser for a top and pulled out the first one I got my hands on, a worn red T-shirt. Seeing what I'd yanked out at random, I pressed the tattered shirt to my face as my eyes welled up. The T-shirt was Josh's. I'd forgotten that I still had it. I inhaled deeply, hoping that a trace of him still lingered on the shirt, but it just smelled like laundry detergent. I knew I should have shoved it back into the dresser or, better yet, thrown it in the trash, but I pulled it over my head, wrapped my arms around my chest, and hugged the fabric against me.

I flipped on the computer, sat on the bed, and checked Facebook. I'd been out of the Facebook loop for a long time; I'd barely checked in since Josh had left. Despite having blocked all of his attempts to contact me, I hadn't had the heart to remove him from my list of friends. I clicked on his name and saw my chef's profile picture, a gorgeous shot of him with a ridiculously perfect ocean behind him, a photo obviously taken in Hawaii. His tanned face smiled at me, and I stuck my tongue out at him. When I browsed through a bunch of photos from Hawaii, it seemed to me that he had been having a jolly good time there frolicking on the beach with new friends, slinging back drinks on a lanai, and snorkeling off a boat in stupendous waters. Ugh, and there were lots of stupid, bikini-clad bronze goddesses in the pictures. I scoffed at the photos but felt pasty and bloated at the sight of those girls.

When my cell rang, I haphazardly picked it up. "Hello?" I said, still staring at a glistening Josh emerging from the water after his first attempt at surfing.

"Chloe, it's Kyle."

I decided right away that I'd make no mention of the nastiness with his father. If Kyle wanted to bring it up, I'd certainly be there for him, but I was in no mood to exercise my social-work skills. "Hey, Kyle."

"Hey yourself. Do you want to try another restaurant tonight? I found this great-looking Cajun place tucked be-tween an all-night laundromat and a goth bar."

"That sounds great," I lied, "but could we do it another night? I've got so much schoolwork to catch up on." Truth-fully, I didn't feel like spending another night out at a bad restaurant. Kyle just didn't seem to know how to pick good ones. But our project was evidently still on.

"Of course. I know I've been asking for a lot of your time lately. Maybe Adrianna is free? And Owen, of course? They might like to have dinner out."

"That's a great idea," I murmured as I glared at a photo of Josh in between two brunettes. "It's really generous. But I just talked to Owen, and Ade is taking Patrick to some moms' group tonight, and Owen is chained to the computer to look for a new job."

"He's giving up on the seafood business?" Kyle asked.

"Apparently. If he can find something better, which at this point could be almost anything." I paused. "Your father can't go with you?" I suggested tentatively.

"My father is having dinner with someone else tonight." He dropped the name of a very famous Food Network chef. I was duly impressed.

"You weren't invited?"

"No, I wasn't." Kyle couldn't hide his bitterness. "Any-way, I think I'll go out and try this place by myself. If it's worth it, then maybe you'll come back with me another night?"

"Definitely."

"Now, you sure I can't lure you away from work? A little gumbo? Creole? Etouffée?"

I had no appetite for anything but soothing ice cream right now. "Sorry. But another night, I promise. I'll talk to you soon."

I hung up and clicked back to Josh's profile page. One of my favorite things about Facebook is being able to see what friends are doing. When Facebook offers me the fill-in-the-blank opportunity to tell people what I'm up to myself— *Chloe* followed by a space to enter whatever I like—I usually update my status by supplying silly things like "*Chloe* is considering buying a BeDazzler so she can stud all her clothes with rhinestones" or "*Chloe* is wondering why she has the theme from *Superman* running through her head."

Josh's status had been updated twenty minutes earlier: "*Josh* is still missing her."

My cell rang again. I figured that Kyle was calling back to reel off more Cajun cooking terms and repeat his invitation to go out. I was wrong.

"You picked up this time," Josh said.

"It was an accident." I clicked off his profile and hit the Status Updates button, the one that let me know what all of my online friends were doing at that Facebook moment.

"What are you doing right now?" he asked.

"Looking through Facebook. Isn't that exciting? My life is terribly scintillating. No wonder you moved to Hawaii."

"Don't say that."

Both of us were silent, but I stared at the computer screen as Josh's status update changed:

Josh is on the phone with the most beautiful girl in the world.

Josh is sorry. He made a huge mistake.

Josh is outside a brown house in Brighton.

Josh is walking up her back stairs.

Josh is hoping against hope that she'll let him inside.

Josh is totally and completely in love.

My hands started to shake. I walked slowly from the bedroom into the living room and looked down at the floor for a moment before lifting my head to the window on the back door. Josh waved his BlackBerry at me. I dropped my phone.

Josh and I locked eyes, and I rushed forward and opened the door. It didn't matter to me at all that I had on crummy clothes or that my hair was in a ratty ponytail or that I was wearing his old shirt—in a desperate attempt to feel close to him. He stepped inside, putting his body inches from mine, and shut the door behind him.

Josh slid an arm around my waist and pulled me against him. "I love you," he breathed. Everything became blurry as he slowly kissed me.

I pulled back slightly. "I don't love you," I said, and then took his face in my hands and kissed him hard.

"But I still love you," he whispered, walking me backward toward the bedroom.

"But I still don't love you," I whispered back, smiling and fumbling to pull off his shirt. "I don't love you at all."

NINETEEN

A good hour later, I rolled onto my side while Josh held me in his arms and kissed my shoulder. It felt as if no time had passed since the last time we'd made love, but I was keenly aware that everything was different now.

"Josh?"

"Yeah, babe," he said as he ran soft kisses across my skin.

"What about Georgie?" I shut my eyes, waiting for his answer.

"What do you mean?"

I sighed and scooted away. "I know you're together, Josh. You and Georgie."

Josh rolled me onto my back and laughed. "Have you totally lost your mind since I've been gone?"

My expression became serious. "Actually, yes."

He hung his head. "I'm sorry. But what would give you the idea that I'm with Snacker's girlfriend? I talked to Owen before I called you, and he told me that you had this crazy notion that I'd hooked up with that girl. There is no truth to that idea whatsoever." Josh slid his body on top of mine and brushed the hair from my face. "None at all."

"But I saw you two together. Last Friday." I didn't particularly want to reveal that I'd been hiding behind a potted plant, spying on him. "I just happened to be coming out of the ladies' room when you told her how hot she was. Not that she isn't, but . . ."

"You nut!" Josh said with a smile. "Didn't you notice that a lot of the food that night was lukewarm when it got to the table?"

"Yeah."

"I was taking Georgie and all the other servers to task for ruining the food. They were all so incompetent. They kept letting the plates sit too long before taking them to the tables."

"Oh." I gazed into his blue eyes and gently ran my hand down his back. "So you're not interested in Georgie?"

"God no. There is only one woman I'm interested in, Chloe."

"Oh," I said again.

"But you're right about one thing. Georgie is not above cheating on Snacker."

"I know. Digger, right?"

"Yeah. How'd you know that?"

"That was another conversation that I happened to overhear."

"My, you heard a lot that night, didn't you?" Josh teased. "I can tell you that Digger wasn't the only guy she was cheating on Snacker with. I never thought Snacker would be the faithful one in a relationship, but he seems really into her. I feel bad for him, although he's probably earned it after all the messing around he's done in his life."

"You don't think . . . you don't think that Snacker could have . . ." I started.

"No. Snacker did not kill Digger." Josh shook his head.

"Did Snacker know that his girlfriend was having an affair with Digger, his close friend? No one—not even Snacker, who has his own knack for philandering—would like that."

"I can't believe that he would ever do something so gruesome. He loved Digger, just like I did."

"He did benefit from Digger's death, though. He got the executive chef job at the Penthouse."

"I hate to admit it, but Snacker's not the most honest, upright person I know, and yes, he did need the money. But that's all."

"Do you know he stole some of your recipes? You couldn't have missed the spring rolls he put on the menu. He thought you'd be in Hawaii and you'd never know."

"No, no." Josh shook his head. "Snacker didn't steal my recipes. After Digger died, Snacker asked me to help him with the menu. I gave him a ton of help, so of course the menu had my mark on it. I don't mind if I give my permission, so it's not like he was being sneaky or anything. Besides, after the opening, Snacker told me that he couldn't handle being the executive chef there. He's going to step down as soon as they find a replacement. He's not ready, and he knows it. He never wanted that job, Chloe."

"Good. What about Digger's girlfriend, Ellie? After all, Digger betrayed her with her best friend. She did seem totally devoted to him."

"Hmm." Josh rolled off me and propped himself up on his elbow while he traced a finger over my stomach. "That's actually a possibility."

"I was the one who had to tell Ellie about Digger's death, and she took it really hard. She was genuinely upset and heartbroken. She asked me to call Georgie. Ellie was obviously on good terms with her friend then. Or she was pretending to be. I know that she went through Digger's e-mail after he died, but she could have done the same thing before his death and found out that he was cheating on her with Georgie. I think she took Digger's laptop from his apartment after the fire," I said, remembering the clean, soot-free outline that I'd seen on the desk. "When she told me that she hadn't been there, she lied."

"She's a better suspect than Snacker, that's for sure. Listen, Chloe," Josh said, turning my face to his. "I have to talk to you about Kyle. I don't know how involved you are with him, but—"

"I'm not involved with him at all, Josh. Not like that. I'm just his cookbook assistant."

"Really? That's a relief. I thought you two were . . ."

"I guess that's what I wanted you to think." I was not about to confess that I had, in fact, made an idiotic play for Kyle and been rebuffed. "It's just that after you left, well, I was pissed. Actually, I'm still pissed. This," I said, waving a finger between us, "is the result of temporary insanity."

"Don't say that. Please don't say this is temporary." Josh leaned down and kissed my stomach, and I let him work his way up to my lips.

"Last August you were only thinking about yourself and what you wanted. You didn't stop and think about what leaving would mean for me. You left me, Josh. Don't forget that." I might have been talking tough, but I felt anything but.

"I left, yes, but I didn't mean to leave you. I know that sounds stupid, but it's true. And I wasn't thinking about myself. Okay, not just about myself. I really thought you'd want to come with me. The couple I work for put me up in this great guesthouse, I looked up a program where you could have kept going to school, and I just . . . I don't know. I thought after the year we'd had that maybe it would be good to get away for a while. To go somewhere where we could just relax and enjoy each other. But you just said no so quickly . . . I screwed up, Chloe. I really screwed up."

"It was escaping, Josh. That's all it was. Going to Hawaii meant avoiding everything here instead of tackling problems head-on. How were things supposed to become normal if we ran off?"

"Babe, what's wrong with escaping once in a while?"

It was true that Josh had had good reason to escape. Josh and I had been madly in love, so that part of my year had been great, but chaos had sullied much of our time together.

Its principal source had been his work. As a chef, he'd worked hideously long hours in return for terrible pay and little appreciation. Most of all, he'd had all-around crummy bosses.

"I didn't know that you'd looked into schools for me," I said. "But you wanted me to just up and leave my life here! Leave Ade, Owen, and Patrick . . ." I trailed off. Adrianna had pointed out to me that, as much as they loved me, they could certainly function without me. "I mean, I have responsibilities here. I have school. I have . . . I have responsibilities. Big responsibilities. Of all sorts!"

Josh nodded. I could tell that he was trying not to smile. "I know. I didn't mean for you to think that I don't take your life seriously or that I don't respect everything you have going on in Boston. You've worked really hard in school, and I'm proud of how much you've put into it. I was just hoping that you would've continued in Hawaii. You know, I found this great community center not too far from where I live. They have a program for underprivileged children, and I talked to the dean at the grad school nearby, and he said they'd consider letting students do internships there, and—"

"You talked to the dean?" I sat up in bed, totally surprised.

"Have you really not read any of my e-mails? Even the Facebook ones?"

"Well, no. I deleted all the ones you sent at first, and then after that, I blocked your address." I hung my head, slightly embarrassed. "I guess I forgot about Facebook."

"Go look. Right now."

I leaned off the bed, pulled my laptop onto my lap, and checked my inbox. Oh my God! There were twenty-six messages, all from Josh. I started at the beginning and skimmed over the screen as my vision became blurry with tears. There were long e-mails in which Josh poured his heart out, begging me to forgive him for leaving and insisting that he still loved me. I tapped through message after message as Josh stroked my back and rubbed his cheek against my arm. What if I had read these messages earlier? Would things have changed? No, I told myself. Last summer, I wasn't ready to up and leave. And who knew if I would ever be ready. I had worked so hard to build an independent life for myself, and I wasn't about to chuck it for some guy. But Josh wasn't just any guy. I promised myself that I'd read Josh's letters more thoroughly later, but there was a limit to how much I could absorb right now.

"Seems like you made a lot of friends in Hawaii," I said as I pulled up the gaggle of girls on the screen. "Lots of very sexy, scantily clad friends."

"That," he said pointing to one of the girls, "is my friend Fritz's fiancée, and that's her cousin, who is married." Josh shut off the computer and took my hands in his. "Since the day I met you, I have not even glanced at another woman. Not one. I don't want anyone else. I don't love anyone else. Only you. Do you believe that?"

I wanted to believe him, but what was the point? He would go back to Hawaii soon, and I'd still be in Boston.

"I'm starving," I announced.

Josh laughed. "Of course you are. Some things never change."

"And some things do," I said pointedly.

"Let's get some food in you and see how you feel after that. You want to walk down to Pino's?"

I couldn't say no to the best, gooiest pizza in the world. "Sure."

After all, I'd worked up quite an appetite. . . .

TWENTY

WHILE we got dressed, Josh brought up Kyle again. "Aside from wanting to see you tonight, I did want to warn you about Kyle. I'm glad you're not dating him, but I don't think you should be working with him, either."

"Why not?" I yanked a sweatshirt over my head and slipped back into my sweatpants. "What exactly is your problem with him?"

"You told me you were working on a cookbook, but I didn't realize it was with Kyle until I saw you with him at the Penthouse. Digger and I went to culinary school with him."

"Owen just told me that this afternoon. I don't know why Kyle never mentioned that he'd trained as a chef, though."

I grabbed my winter boots and ski jacket, and took my keys off the desk. "You ready?"

Josh nodded. "I'll tell you why Kyle never told you. He dropped out of the program."

"He did?" We went out the back door. It was dark now. I held the railing as I walked down the stairs.

"Yeah, and Digger and I are probably to blame for that. Kyle just couldn't cook. He was awful. He couldn't tell good food from bad. He dropped stuff all the time, never cleaned his workstation, burned things more times than I could count—he was just incompetent in every aspect." Josh put his arm around my shoulder as we walked, and I unconsciously leaned into him. It was bitterly cold out. "He basically was lazy and a big baby. He couldn't take the competitive environment at school. He hated the rough atmosphere and the constant pranks and jokes we all used to pull. Honestly, that made us ride him even harder, and we called him on all of his screwups. Look, it wasn't nice of us, but we were young, and he was such an easy target."

"So you were a bully?"

"I guess so," Josh admitted. "And I did try to smooth things over with him, but he didn't want anything to do with me. Honestly, all he did was complain and try to get us to cover up his mistakes or outright do his work for him. He was a pill. And he was always going out with these glamorous, attractive women. He thought he was so cool because he dated girls who looked like beauty-pageant queens. We teased him about that, too. Don't think for a second that you're going to get any credit for this cookbook. He's going to say that he did all the work. That is, if he doesn't ruin it completely."

"You sound like Kyle's father. You know who that is, right? Hank Boucher."

"I know. His whack job of a father is the other reason he quit school. Just before Hank was coming to visit Kyle at school, Digger and I teased him to pieces about what we were going to do when his father the famous chef got there. That we'd make sure Hank knew how terrible his son was doing as a culinary student and all that. I know, I know," Josh said when I glared at him, "it was wrong, and we were obnoxious punks back then. But Kyle wanted a free pass in life because of who his father was, and the whole time he couldn't so much as boil water without setting fire to the entire stove top! Kyle was so bullshit with us and so scared of his father finding out what a dink he was that he up and dropped out of school just before his father arrived. Kyle didn't like me much, obviously, but he really loathed Digger, because Digger was the one who instigated the majority of the teasing. Kyle totally wanted to kill him most of the time."

I stopped in my tracks, yanking Josh backward. "Oh my God."

"What?"

"Digger was killed just before Kyle and Hank were supposed to meet him at his apartment for a tasting. I don't think it was a coincidence." I looked right at Josh. "I think Kyle never wanted Hank and Digger to meet."

"Oh God." Josh dropped his head and put his hands on his hips. "You could be right. Kyle might have killed Digger. Damn it! But we don't have any proof. We have nothing."

"And Kyle called me before you showed up tonight to see if I wanted to go out to dinner with him. I never want to see him again! And when I said I was busy, he asked if Adrianna and Owen might want to go. Thank God Ade is out with Patrick tonight, and Owen's at home job hunting. I'm not letting anyone I know anywhere near Kyle again. Ever!"

"Chloe, Adrianna is exactly Kyle's type. She should be careful," he warned. "Back when we were in school, he tried to compensate for his total incompetence in school by showing off his gorgeous women and bragging about them every chance he got. Maybe he's changed, but I doubt it."

"Kyle told me that his father has been married to one trophy wife after another. Like father, like son, I guess." I looped my arm through Josh's and continued walking. "You know, Kyle did invite Adrianna along with us to dinner quite a bit. But I just thought . . . Oh, it's stupid, but I thought that he was a nice guy who wanted to get to know my friends. He seemed to feel bad that she and Owen have been struggling so much, and he liked to treat her to dinner. But this whole time he's been interested in her?"

"He can be smooth when he wants to," Josh said. "There's got to be a way to link Kyle to the fire at Digger's apartment, but I can't think on an empty stomach. Let's get some dinner, and we'll figure something out."

"Why don't we swing by Owen and Ade's and see if Owen wants to come out with us. I know he's supposed to be on the computer all night, but I think we should tell him what we know about Kyle as soon as possible."

"Good idea."

We walked silently for a few minutes. When we got close to Adrianna and Owen's apartment, I couldn't help sniffing. "Ugh! Owen must be grilling again. Only that nut would stand outside in this cold just to burn chicken."

"I don't think that smell is from a grill." Josh walked quickly now, pulling me forward. "Come on."

"What do you mean?" I asked as I hurried alongside him. Looking up at the three-story building, I saw nothing alarming. Still, there was no denying that the burning smell was growing stronger. I immediately flashed back to my malodorous trek through Digger's apartment. The one odd thing about the building was the absence of lighted windows. The windows on the first two floors were understandably dark since the owners, who lived there, were away, but Ade and Owen's third-floor apartment was dark, too. Owen was supposed to be at home conducting an online job search, so there should have been lights on, I reasoned; Owen wasn't the kind of person who huddles over a computer in a darkened room. "This way," I said to Josh as I started across the lawn toward the back of the building, where I expected to look up and see Owen hovering over a smoldering grill on the wooden fire escape—in other words, taking advantage of Ade's absence to do exactly what she'd told him not to do. As for the stench, he'd probably run out of lighter fluid and was burning random items in an attempt to ignite the charcoal.

But I was wrong.

"Jesus Christ!" said Josh, panicked.

I looked up to the top of the fire escape. Like the windows visible from the front of the building, those at the back of the building were dark, but light from the house next door showed heavy smoke billowing from inside Ade and Owen's apartment. Owen was nowhere in sight. "Owen!" I screamed. "Owen!"

Josh rushed forward and started to climb the fire escape. "Call nine-one-one!" he yelled.

I fumbled in my pocket for my cell as I ran to the front of the house, where the streetlights would let me see the buttons on the phone. Once I reached the sidewalk, I dialed 911 and, pressing the cell to my ear, ran up the front steps in the hope that Ade or Owen had for some reason left the door unlocked. No such luck. I had a key to their apartment, but it was on its own key ring at my condo. Why hadn't I just attached it to my key ring? Owen had probably passed out from smoke inhalation and couldn't hear Josh's and my screams. I frantically shouted Ade and Owen's address into the phone and, instead of listening to what the operator said, felt compelled to keep repeating the address at top volume, as if loudly reiterating the information would somehow speed the arrival of fire trucks. Too frightened to listen, I barely heard what the operator said but was left with the impression that help was, or would be, on the way. After again trying the front door and even banging on it and kicking it, I returned to the sidewalk just as Josh came around to the front of the building.

He shook his head. "I almost got up there, but there's too much smoke." He reeked of it. He had his jacket slung over one arm. I knew without asking that he'd taken it off and used it to cover his nose and mouth in an effort to penetrate the smoke. "You tried the front door?"

I nodded and shoved my key ring at him. "Run to my place and get their key. It's on top of the TV. Go!"

Josh took off running while I continued screaming for Owen.

Suddenly there was someone standing next to me. "I had no idea you were so desperate to see me, Chloe."

"Owen!" I cried and threw my arms around him. He was perfectly safe and not lying on his apartment floor dying! "Thank God!"

"What's all the fuss? And what the hell is that nasty smell?"

"Your apartment is on fire! Thank God you're safe! I thought you were up there. Josh tried to get in the back way, but he couldn't. I'm just glad no one is home." I let out a massive sigh of relief.

Owen's face grew rigid. "Ade and Patrick are in there!" He flew to the front door and patted down his pockets. "I don't have my key! I don't have my key!" He jerked the doorknob back and forth and kicked the door repeatedly, but the old, heavy door didn't budge. "Adrianna!" he started screaming. "Her group got cancelled. She's probably in bed sleeping. Oh God!"

"Josh is getting my key right now. I called nine-one-one." I felt sick and panicked. My best friend and my godson were trapped inside, burning to death! As Owen continued to pound on the door, I looked around frantically. I couldn't just stand here and wait for the fire trucks. I had to do something! There were no ladders lying around, but maybe someone had left a garden hose out back. By this time of year, hoses should've been put away for the winter, but I was still going to look. I flew into the backyard again and, in the light from the next house, searched the foundation for a water spigot. I found it. But there was no hose. Shit! Shit! I glanced up to the third floor and choked on a sob. The smoke was getting heavier.

Without thinking, I ran to the fire escape and started up the stairs, tripping several times. My legs were shaking so violently that I could barely put one foot in front of the other without catching the toe of my boot on a stair. "Adrianna!" I cried out through my tears. Pausing on the second-floor landing, I called her name more forcibly. I had to make her hear me! I had to! I caught sight of the first visible flame as it shot from the living room window. "No!" I screamed. "No! Adrianna! Adrianna!"

Like my condo building, this house was wooden—a tinderbox. That first flame would spread in no time. I cursed the wooden fire escape, which was as vulnerable to fire as the building itself. I'd have to descend almost immediately. Still, I continued screaming for my friend and praying that Josh would return or that the fire trucks would arrive. It couldn't have been more than a few minutes since I'd called, but it felt like an eternity.

Owen's small grilling area above me was rapidly disintegrating as the fire began to grow. When a burning piece of wood dropped next to me, I kicked it off the landing, threw my arms over my head, and screamed with everything that I had in me. "Adrianna!"

"Chloe!" The male voice came from below.

I glanced down. Even in my petrified state, I was stunned. "Kyle? What—?"

My cookbook partner stood at the base of the fire escape. "Chloe, what are you doing? Get down! Get off there now!" He took a step onto the wooden stairs.

"Get away from me!" I hollered as I moved up to the next step. "You did this! You started this fire, didn't you?" I yanked my arms out of my coat and threw it over my head in the hope of protecting myself from any more falling debris. Kyle scrambled higher until he was only a few steps away. I couldn't go up any farther. "Josh!" I screamed. "Owen! Help me! Help me!"

"Chloe, you have to get down from there!" Kyle begged.

"Don't get any closer to me, you psycho!" I swung my leg out as a warning. "Ade and Patrick are in there!"

"What? No! No!" He froze and stared at me, his head shaking back and forth. "Adrianna!"

Kyle lunged past me, knocking me to the side. I grabbed the railing and caught myself just before I toppled down the stairs. Frightened of Kyle and knowing that I was unable to save Adrianna and Patrick, I made my way downward. As I descended, the wail of sirens finally began to fill the air. Reaching the ground, I backed up and watched as Kyle reached the stairs to the third floor, the stairs that led to Ade and Owen's landing. He coughed over and over as smoke swirled around him, and then he suddenly leaped the stairs, two at a time, to reach what was left of the landing and the back door.

"Kyle!" I yelled uselessly.

He blindly shot an arm forward to touch the door and screamed in pain, fell backward, and hit the railing behind him. Within a fraction of a second, the railing, none too sturdy to begin with, gave way, and Kyle plummeted three stories down and hit the ground. Feeling sick and sickeningly overwhelmed, I turned away.

Josh's voice rang out over the sirens. I turned to see him jogging up the lawn toward me. "We got them! We got Ade and Patrick!"

"Are they okay?"

"I think so. Yeah." Josh wrapped both arms around me and pulled me against him. "It's all okay now."

I clung to him tightly and buried my face in his chest. Nobody in the world could make me feel as safe and as right as Josh could. God, I had missed this feeling. "But, Josh. Look." I pulled away and walked slowly toward Kyle. He'd landed on his back. Blood seeped from his nose and from the side of his head, and his legs were splayed at awkward angles. As I watched, he turned his head slightly; miraculously, he was alive, although maybe not for long. "Josh, get the EMTs."

Josh nodded and took off. I knelt down next to Kyle and spread my coat across him. He was mouthing something, struggling to speak. I leaned my ear close to him.

Kyle looked up at the sky and blinked rapidly. "It wasn't supposed to be them, you know. Right? It was supposed to be Owen. We could have been together. I could have made her happier than he could. I'd have taken care of her. You'd have taken Patrick. I know you would. You love him. You'd have been the perfect mother."

"Just hold on, Kyle," I said evenly.

"See, Dad?" he continued. "Now I have the wife, the beautiful wife, and cookbook, and nobody is going to ruin it this time."

"You started the fire at Digger's, didn't you?" I asked softly, leadingly.

"Oh, I had to. Hank Boucher wouldn't have liked what Digger had to say about me." His lips curled into a small smile. "That wouldn't have worked out at all. I think I need to rest now."

And with that, Kyle's head rocked to the side. I pulled the coat up over his face and walked away.

TWENTY-ONE

"WHERE'S Patrick? Who has my baby?"

"He's right here," I said gently. "I've got him. He's fine."
I carried Patrick out from my bedroom and handed him to
Adrianna.

"Sorry. I'm sorry. I'm still freaked out." Adrianna reached
out and took Patrick from my arms. She tightened the blanket around her son and kissed the top of his head. "Thanks
for letting us crash here, Chloe. Obviously we can't live in
that house any time soon."

"I doubt you'll ever be moving back in there, Ade." I put
my hand on her shoulder and leaned in to give her a hug.

"True. This is the opportunity that our landlords have
been looking for. A good excuse to renovate the apartments

back into a single-family house. I don't know where we'll go."

"We'll find you guys something. How are you feeling?" I asked. I couldn't hide my concern. "I know the hospital wanted you two to stay only one night, but I can't help worrying."

Ade shrugged. "We're fine. Physically, that is. I'm still in a bit of shock, though. I had no idea that Kyle was such a whack job."

I nodded. Ade and Patrick were lucky to have needed only minor treatment for smoke inhalation. By the time Josh had returned from my condo with the key to Ade and Owen's apartment, the fire had really picked up. Only then had the smoke alarm gone off. One of the firefighters told Owen that some smoke alarms are triggered by flames and not by smoke. Ade might have been in the deep, exhausted sleep of a new mother, or she might already have been suffering from smoke inhalation when the alarm finally had sounded. In either case, I was immensely relieved that nothing worse had happened.

"So, Kyle wanted me?" Ade squirmed uncomfortably and pulled Patrick closer. "And he started the fire believing that Owen was inside?"

"Yes. It seems that Kyle imagined that with Owen out of the way, you could be together. He took all of the things you'd been saying about Owen's job and terrible pay and wanting a better place to live, and twisted them in his mind. He developed the idea that he was exactly what you were really looking for and that he'd get rid of Owen for you so you two could, I don't know, run off into the sunset together."

Ade shut her eyes and shivered. Patrick let out a small squawk, as if he were in tune with his mother's emotions. "Sick man." She gently stroked the baby's back.

"He thought that you were out that night and that Owen was home because that's what I'd told him when he called me earlier in the day. He broke the glass in the door by the fire escape and started the fire using charcoal and lighter fluid that he tossed inside and on the fire escape itself."

"God, and then he watched the fire from the backyard?" She pulled Patrick in even tighter.

"I know. But I guess he wanted to watch. Some fire-setters do."

"Do you think Kyle had been waiting for an opportunity to kill Owen?"

"I'm not sure. I don't even think that his fixation on you had all that much to do with you. I think that it was all about his crazy father. He set the fire at Digger's the night before Hank Boucher was going to meet Digger for the first time and hear what an utter failure his son had been in culinary school. The night of your fire—"

"Don't call it my fire," Ade said. "It's Kyle's fire."

"Sorry, the night Kyle set your place on fire, he'd just been dealt another rejection from his father, and I think that it triggered another desperate and pathological reaction. Kyle was determined to create the ideal-looking family that he thought he should have—the beautiful wife and the cookbook accomplishment—and when Hank didn't invite his own son to this prestigious dinner, it set him off. His fire-setting was more about his anger and his fear of his father than anything else."

I immediately thought of Danny, my client, and realized how deep his rage must be at his own awful father. I would have to insist that Danny make some changes; I didn't know whether it would be possible to get his father to come to a session. If not, my client would still have to disengage from his father and deal with the damage that had been done. I had only a month left with Danny until my six-week winter break, so I made a mental note to meet with my supervisor and come up with a solid plan for continued treatment with one of the senior therapists. And then there was Alison and her fantasies about leaving her boyfriend for an idealized man who was never going to love her.

As the parallels between my clients and Kyle became obvious, it dawned on me that I'd left my client notes on the coffee table when Kyle had been at my place. What's more, when I'd moved my notes out of the way, he'd joked about my not wanting him to read my diary. He'd read about Alison, client A, who was desperately in love with an older man and wanted to leave her current partner for this new, suave, charming man. Kyle must have thought that my notes about A were about Adrianna and about her infatuation with him! God, this should teach me to keep my notes hidden!

The first thing that I'd done after coming home from the hospital was to pack up all of the cookbook materials and mail them to Hank Boucher. I wanted nothing to do with that man ever again. I'd turned off the ringer on the phone, and I'd refused to turn on the television or the computer or to look at a newspaper, since I knew that the headlines would be riddled with the story of famous chef Hank

Boucher's murderous son. Today, I wanted to focus solely on my friends.

"Look, Ade, you can all stay here for as long as you like. I can go crash at my parents' house in Newton for a while. It's not a problem."

"Absolutely not. We're not about to kick you out of your own home, Chloe," she protested.

"You're not kicking me out. I'm volunteering. In fact, I'm insisting. I'll be perfectly fine at my parents' place."

Ade brightened. "Really? I hate to put you out of your own apartment, Chloe, but I don't know what other options we have. And we lost so much of what little we had. Even the stuff that wasn't actually burned reeks of smoke. Hopefully we can salvage most of our clothes and linens with a few good runs in the washing machine, but . . . so much is gone. The only thing that really matters, though, is that Owen, Patrick, and I are still together." She leaned down and kissed Patrick's forehead and rubbed her nose against his. "When I think about what could have happened, what we could have lost, I just . . . it's just unbearable to even consider. Thank God we're all okay." Ade repositioned herself on the couch so that Patrick lay across her knees, gazing adoringly at his mother. "You sure about letting us crash here?"

"Of course you're staying here. My mother will be thrilled to have me home for a while, too. And speaking of Owen, he and Josh should be back from your apartment soon with some of your things."

"And speaking of Josh," Ade said raising her eyebrows, "what were you two doing together the other night, huh? Gimme the scoop."

"We were just, ah, well . . . See, we met up to talk about Kyle, and then . . ."

Adrianna stared at me while I stuttered helplessly.

"Okay, fine!" I tossed my hands up. "Here's what happened." I relayed all the juicy details from my pre-fire evening with Josh.

"You slept together? Yahoo! So what's going to happen now?" she asked excitedly, jostling Patrick as she sat upright. "Does this mean you're finally back together? Everything is finally back to normal, and he's moving back to Boston?"

"I don't really know what it means, but no, he's not coming back here. We're supposed to talk later today. He's flying to Hawaii tomorrow morning."

"Well, you can't let him, Chloe! You can't! You love each other! He wrote you all those romantic letters that you never read because you're a moron!"

"Thank you very much," I snarled.

"You know what I mean," she said more calmly. "You need to make this work out. I mean, really. Look what just happened to me. Life is too damn short. Get your man back."

I sighed and shook my head. "It's so much more complicated than that. How are we supposed to make it work out? He'll be in Hawaii, and I'll be here. Besides, I'm still angry with him for leaving in the first place. He left me, Ade. I'm no freaking Carrie from *Sex and the City*. Josh is not my Mr. Big. Letters? He has to do better than that."

"You listen to me, Chloe," Adrianna said forcefully. "Get over it. You hear me? Get over it. Josh messed up. Big time.

He really messed up, and he knows it. Honey, people make mistakes, and Josh made an enormous mistake. But like he told you, he needed to get away from the restaurant scene here. It was consuming him and draining him and making him miserable. We all saw what he was going through, and it sucked for him. So maybe he did the wrong thing by leaving Boston, but I can understand why he needed to get out of here, can't you?"

I closed my eyes for a second and clenched my jaw. "Yeah," I admitted. "I can. Do you know what he told me this morning at the hospital? He said that he loves this personal-chef job more than he thought he would, and he can't imagine ever working in a restaurant again. I know that he doesn't want to come back to Boston anytime soon. He's happy where he is."

"See? He needed to make some major life changes."

"Including getting rid of me? He made his life changes, and now he can live with them."

"No, that's not fair. You are one part of his life, a big part, but only one part. If the rest of his life is in the crapper, how is he supposed to make you happy when everything else sucks? He had to get his work life straightened out for himself, and that's allowed. He screwed up, he paid the price, and now it's time to forgive him. You made your point, now get over it and quit punishing him. And yourself. You don't get that may shots at real love."

"I had it once. I'm sure I'll find it again," I said as dismissively as possible.

"Don't be so cavalier about this," Ade warned.

"I'm not being cavalier, but I worked hard to feel as independent as I do and to finally feel connected to school and becoming a social worker. For the first time, I am actually looking forward to graduating in May and getting a job. I think I could be good at this work. I don't need a man! I can be happy and fulfilled with my friends, my family, and whatever great job I get."

Adrianna sighed with exasperation. "I don't know how you started equating independence with not having a relationship, dummy. You can do both. You can be a strong, savvy woman and still be in love. Don't be stupid, Chloe. You have six weeks of vacation coming up."

"So?"

"So go to Hawaii!"

"No," I shook my head. "I'm not going to Hawaii. I have things to do here."

"They can wait."

"I have a whole semester of classes coming up," I protested.

"You'll be back for those. And then you'll graduate, and you can do whatever you want then. You can be with Josh if you want to, Chloe. You love Josh."

"I don't love Josh. Josh is my past. He really is. I loved him. Loved what we had, but it's over. It is over." I swallowed hard.

"You're being stubborn."

"I'm not being stubborn. I'm being independent."

Adrianna flopped back on the couch with Patrick and looked at her baby. "She's being stubborn."

TWENTY-TWO

MY mother was a little disappointed that I hadn't gone home to stay with her, but she understood. I'd found a better place to spend my winter break.

When I arrived at the cottage, I explained who I was, and the woman who owned it smiled and let me in. I liked her immediately. She was a joyful woman who seemed to have no cares in the world. "Make yourself at home. I'm so glad you're here," she said cheerfully. "There is a refreshment for you in the refrigerator. My specialty." She smiled and winked before leaving me alone.

I peered into the fridge. Before helping myself to a mai tai, I unpacked. While putting some things away in a dresser, I noticed that two of the four drawers were empty.

I hung a dress in the closet; the clothes were all pushed to one side, and empty hangers occupied the other. The left side of the bathroom vanity was empty. I stowed my makeup and hair products there. I opened the sliding glass door and took a deep breath, closing my eyes. It's always kind of hard settling in, figuring out what to do first: put this and that away, just sit down and pour a drink, or call my mother or Ade. I was overwhelmed—but in a good way. And for the first time in a very long time, I suddenly felt all of the muscles in my neck and shoulders relax. Paradise.

I walked back inside, knowing that it wouldn't be long. I went to the fridge, took out the pitcher of mai tais, and poured two.

Then I got naked. Almost.

Josh opened the door to the guesthouse and, with his back to me, tossed his keys on the table and threw a wet towel into the laundry basket. He had on swim trunks, and his hair was still wet.

"How's the water?" I asked.

Josh whipped around. He stared at me for a moment, his jaw dropped, and then he grinned. "The water is perfect." Still smiling, he put his hands on his hips. "Are you really here, or am I having another one of my fantasies? God, you are beautiful."

I handed him a mai tai. "Come find out. Dream or reality?" We clinked our glasses together. I laughed and beckoned him to the bed. "I was under the *Fantasy Island* impression that everyone was given a lei when getting off the plane, but I had to buy mine." I touched a finger to one of the flowers around my neck.

"If I'd known you were coming, I'd have been waiting for you with an armful of leis. But considering that's all you're wearing, I think you chose well. The colors look good on you." He winked and moved closer, crawling across the bed until his chest was against mine and his hands cradled my head.

"I still don't believe you showed up here," Josh said. "When I said I'd move back to Boston to be together, you said no. Then I must have asked you thirty times to visit me on your break, and you said no every time."

I brushed my hand against his cheek and kissed him softly. "I know that you don't want to be in Boston. At least for now. And you know," I said casually, "I couldn't think of anything better to do over break."

"Very funny. I'll try to keep you entertained." Josh kissed me. "I can't wait to show you around. You're going to love it here."

"I think I just might." I smiled at him. God, he was so much less stressed than I'd ever seen him. It felt wonderful to see how happy he was.

"Are Owen and Adrianna staying at your place?" Josh nuzzled my neck.

"Hmmm," I said as a yes.

"I'm glad they're watching the cats for you."

"Uh-huh." I was getting distracted.

I looked up at my gorgeous chef, the man I loved and who loved me back, and thought about everything that we'd been through in the past year. A Hawaiian escape with Josh had been a pretty good idea. Six weeks of bliss lay ahead of me. Maybe I could find a part-time job while I was here so I could continue paying off those damn bills.

I had one semester of school left and then graduation. Who knows? While I was here, maybe I'd talk to someone at the community center Josh had told me about. But I didn't need to worry about planning too far ahead. I'd know what to do when the time came.

For now, the only thing I had to think about was what I was going to have Josh make me for dinner. . . .

RECIPES

Grilled Ohio Lamb Steak with Cannellini Beans, Anchovy, and Parsley

Jonathon Sawyer, chef at the Greenhouse Tavern
Cleveland, OH
www.thegreenhousetavern.com

Serves 7–10

Lamb Steaks:

1 *whole leg of lamb*
4 *tbsp. extra virgin olive oil*
1 *bulb garlic, smashed with skin still on*

2 *sprigs fresh rosemary, bruised*
   Salt and coarsely ground black pepper to taste

Have your local butcher or chef fabricate the leg of lamb into three sections: shoulder, shank, and steak (steak being the meat in between the shank and shoulder). Reserve the shank and shoulder for another preparation. The steaks should be cut across the leg, bone-in, and 1" to 2" thickness. This will yield 7 to 10 steaks.

Marinate the lamb steaks in the olive oil, garlic, and rosemary.

Season lamb steaks with salt and pepper and grill to desired doneness. Allow to rest for five minutes.

Cannellini Beans:

1 *qt. dried cannellini beans*
6 *qt. water*
2 *cups extra virgin olive oil*
1 *sprig fresh bay leaf*
   Salt to taste

Soak cannellini beans in 4 quarts of water for at least 24 hours. Strain and rinse beans.

In a large, heavy-bottomed stock pot, add beans and cover with water. On high heat, allow beans to come to a boil, then reduce heat to a low simmer. Let the beans cook until wholly cooked through without splitting. The tenderness of the bean is entirely up to you. Carefully remove the beans from the cooking liquid and place them in a sealable container with the olive oil, bay leaf, and a little salt. This will preserve the beans in the oil and allow them to absorb some of the oil. They will keep refrigerated for two weeks.

Salsa Verde:

- *1 bunch parsley, chopped*
- *8 anchovy filets (salt-packed anchovies preferred), rinsed and chopped*
- *1 tbsp. capers (salt-packed capers preferred), rinsed and chopped*
- *3 cloves garlic, chopped*
- *1 tbsp. dried chili flakes*
   Salt and pepper to taste

Combine all ingredients except for the salt and pepper and mix well. Mix the strained, cooked cannellini beans with an equal amount of salsa verde and allow to reach room temperature. Taste for seasoning and add salt and pepper as needed.

To plate:

- *Toasted bread heels or crostini*
- *2 lemons, zested and juiced*
- *1 cup extra virgin olive oil, the highest quality you can afford*

Place some toasted bread heels or crostini on a plate. Place the sliced lamb steak on top (with any juices left over from the resting) and pour the salsa verde and beans over the top. Garnish with lemon zest and extra virgin olive oil.

Shrimp and Brie Purses with Apricot Vinaigrette

Bill Park, sous-chef at LTK Bar and Kitchen
Boston, MA
www.ltkbarandkitchen.com

Serves 4–6

Apricot Vinaigrette:

¼ cup jarred apricot chutney
8 dried cherries
½ cup apple cider vinegar
Salt and pepper
½ cup extra virgin olive oil

Combine all ingredients and set aside.

Salad (per person):

2 oz. arugula
3 apple slices
1 tsp. sliced almonds
5 dried cherries

Toss ingredients with as much vinaigrette as you like and set equal portions on individual plates.

For pastry assembly:

1   *package frozen puff pastry squares, thawed*
1   *wedge Brie, approximately 6–9 oz.*
12 *shrimp, cooked and roughly chopped*
1   *egg, beaten*

Preheat oven to 425 degrees.

Gently roll out each square of puff pastry dough to stretch them a bit. Poke a few holes in each piece with a fork. Place roughly 1½ oz. of Brie in the center of each square and top with 1½ tbsp. of the shrimp. Brush the corners with the egg and then pull the corners to the center and tighten around the middle to form purses.

Set purses on a baking sheet and bake for 12–15 minutes until golden brown. Serve with arugula salad.

Oysters with Asian Pear and Fennel

Bill Park

Serves 4

1   *tbsp. olive oil*
1   *bulb fennel, cored and finely diced*
1   *shallot, finely diced*

1   Asian pear, peeled, cored, finely diced
¼   cup white wine
1   cup heavy cream
½   tsp. turmeric
    Pinch of cayenne
    Salt and pepper to taste
12 Oysters in the shell
    Chopped parsley

Preheat oven to 400 degrees.

Heat the oil in a saucepan and sauté the fennel and shallot until tender. Add the pear and wine and sauté for a couple minutes and then add the cream, turmeric, cayenne, salt, and pepper, and reduce heat and simmer for approximately 10 minutes.

Set whole, unopened oysters on a baking sheet and bake until they pop open, approximately 7 minutes. Remove from the oven, discard the top shells, and top each oyster with a hefty spoonful of the fennel-pear mixture. Garnish each oyster with a bit of parsley before serving.

Seared Scallops on Polenta with Red Pepper and Chive Jam

Bill Park

Serves 20 as passed appetizers

Red Pepper Jam:

2 red peppers, seeded and roughly chopped
2 tbsp. sugar
1 tsp. salt
½ tsp. black pepper

Place peppers in a blender and puree. Set the puree in a saucepan with the sugar, salt, and pepper, and cook over medium heat until almost dry. Cool and reserve.

Polenta:

3 cups chicken broth
2 tbsp. butter
2 cups polenta
1 cup heavy cream
¾ cup shredded Parmesan
Salt and pepper to taste
Olive oil or butter

Heat the chicken broth and butter in a saucepan and bring to a simmer. Slowly add the polenta, stirring constantly. Cook on low heat for 15 minutes, continuing to stir constantly until the polenta has thickened. Add small amounts of cream and cheese, alternating until you have the flavor you want. Season with salt and pepper. The polenta should be very thick. Lay the polenta out on a greased cookie sheet and refrigerate overnight. Cut into 1" X 1" squares and sear in a hot sauté pan with a bit of olive oil or butter until just golden brown on both sides. Reserve unless you are serving right away.

Scallops:

40 *small sea scallops*
    Salt and pepper to taste
    Olive oil
1   *tbsp. butter*

Season the scallops with salt and pepper. Heat olive oil and butter over medium-high heat in a large sauté pan and cook scallops for about three minutes until done.

To plate:

Heat the polenta squares in the oven if needed, then top each with a scallop and a bit of the red pepper jam.

RECIPES

Pumpkin and Apple Bisque
Bill Park

Makes roughly 1 gallon of soup

- 2 *tbsp. olive oil*
- 1 *large Spanish onion, thinly sliced*
- 8 *apples, peeled, cored, and thinly sliced*
- 1 *tsp. allspice*
- 1 *can pumpkin puree*
- 1 *quart chicken broth*
- 1 *pint heavy cream*
  Salt and pepper to taste
- ½ *tsp. cinnamon*
- 2 *tsp. butter*
- 1 *baguette*
  Olive oil as needed for brushing

In a stockpot, heat oil, onion, half of the apples, and allspice and sauté over medium heat until soft. Add the pumpkin puree, chicken broth, and cream and bring to a simmer. Cook for 30 minutes, then season to taste with salt and pepper. In a separate pan, sauté the rest of the apples with the cinnamon and butter over medium heat until the apples are soft. (You may add onions, too, if you like.) Slice baguette on the bias, brush with oil, sprinkle with salt and pepper, and bake or grill until crispy.

Ladle soup into bowls, set a good dollop of the apple mixture into the center, and then set a baguette slice on top of the apple mixture.

Pumpkin Cheesecake Tarts

J. B. Stanley, author of the Supper Club series

www.jbstanley.com

www.cozychicksblog.com

Makes 12 tarts

⅔ *cup crushed gingersnaps*

2 *tbsp. butter, melted*

8 *oz. cream cheese, softened*

1 *cup canned pumpkin*

½ *cup sugar*

1 *tsp. pumpkin pie spice*

1 *tsp. pure vanilla extract*

2 *large eggs, beaten*

  One milk chocolate bar, melted

Preheat oven to 325 degrees.

Line a muffin pan with paper cups (enough for 12 tarts). Combine gingersnap crumbs and butter in a small bowl. Press approximately one tbsp. of the crumb mixture into the bottom of each muffin cup. Use all of the crumb mixture. Bake for five minutes. Beat together cream cheese, pumpkin, sugar, pumpkin pie spice, and vanilla. Add beaten eggs. Pour over baked gingersnap crusts. Bake 25–30 minutes. Drizzle melted milk chocolate over cooled tarts and serve.

RECIPES

Pepper Encrusted Beef Tenderloin with Creamy Horseradish

J. B. Stanley

Serves 4

4 6-oz. *beef tenderloin filets*
¾ tsp. *salt, divided*
1 tbsp. *cracked black peppercorns*
½ cup butter, *divided in half*
2 tsp. *flour*
¼ tsp. *ground pepper*
⅔ cup whipping *cream*
1 tsp. *Dijon mustard*
2 tsp. *prepared horseradish*

Sprinkle filets evenly with ½ tsp. of the salt; press cracked peppercorns on all sides of each filet. Melt ¼ cup of the butter in a large skillet over medium-high heat. Add beef and cook 3–4 minutes on each side or until beef is at desired level of doneness. Melt remaining ¼ cup butter in a saucepan over medium heat. Whisk in flour, remaining ¼ tsp. salt, and ground pepper. Cook for 1 minute. Whisk in whipping cream, mustard, and horseradish. Cook, stirring constantly, until mixture is nice and thick. Dollop over filets or serve on the side in a small bowl.

Aloha Fruit Salad

Mia King, author

www.miaking.com

Serves 6

1 orange, peeled and diced

3 ripe mangoes, pits removed, peeled and sliced

3 bananas, sliced

1 Fuji apple, skin on, cored and sliced

1 small pineapple, sliced (or 1 8-oz. can pineapple chunks)

¼ cup unsweetened coconut, shredded and lightly toasted

¼ cup macadamia nuts or walnuts, lightly toasted and coarsely chopped

½ cup date pieces

3 tbsp. honey

⅓ cup lemon juice

¼ cup pineapple juice (reserve from fresh or canned pineapple) or orange juice

Place the orange, mangoes, bananas, apple, and pineapple in a large bowl. Reserve any pineapple juice; set aside.

Sprinkle the coconut, macadamia nuts, and date pieces on top of the fruit.

In a small bowl, whisk together the honey, lemon juice, and pineapple juice. Drizzle over fruit and serve.

Baked Tomato Nests
Mia King

Serves 4

4 *large tomatoes*
Salt and pepper to taste
4 *large eggs*
4 *tbsp. double cream or heavy cream*
4 *tbsp. grated Parmesan*

Preheat the oven to 350 degrees.

Slice off the tops of the tomatoes. Using a spoon, carefully scoop out the pulp and seeds without piercing the sides. Turn the tomato shells upside down on a paper towel to drain for fifteen minutes.

Turn tomatoes upright and place in an ovenproof dish just large enough to hold them in a single layer. Season the insides with salt and pepper. Carefully break one egg into each tomato shell, then top with 1 tbsp. cream and 1 tbsp. Parmesan.

Bake for 15–20 minutes, or until the eggs are just set. Serve hot.

RECIPES

Stromboli
Mia King

Yields 1 loaf, serves 6–8

Dough:

2   tsp. dry yeast
1¾ cups water (plus extra if needed), divided
3½ cups unbleached flour
1½ tsp. salt
3   tbsp. olive oil

Filling and topping:

14 oz. mozzarella or provolone cheese, cubed
1   garlic clove, peeled and chopped
3   tbsp. olive oil, divided
1   tsp. coarse sea salt
3   sprigs rosemary, stems removed
1   tsp. pepper

Other filling options:

2 tbsp. dried thyme or dried Italian seasoning
1 handful fresh basil leaves
1 cup black olives, chopped
½ cup onion, thinly sliced

RECIPES

Preheat oven to 400 degrees.

Sprinkle yeast in 1 cup of room-temperature water. Leave for 5 minutes, then stir to dissolve.

Mix flour and salt in a large bowl. Make a well in the center and pour in the yeast-and-water mixture and the olive oil. Mix in the flour from the sides, stirring in the reserved water as needed, to form a soft, sticky dough.

Turn the dough out onto a lightly floured work surface. Knead until smooth, silky, and elastic, about 10 minutes.

Place the dough in a clean, oiled bowl and cover with a dish towel. Let rise until doubled in size, about 1½–2 hours. Punch down and chafe (see note) for 5 minutes, and then let the dough rest for 10 minutes.

Shape the dough into a 14" X 8" rectangle. Cover with a dish towel and let rest for 10 minutes.

Spread the cheese, garlic, and anything else you'd like to add evenly over the dough. Roll the dough like a Swiss roll or jellyroll, starting at one of the shorter sides, but don't roll it too tightly. Pinch the edges of the seam and tuck the ends under.

Place on an oiled baking sheet. Use a skewer or carving fork to pierce several holes all the way through the dough to the baking sheet. Sprinkle the top with 1 tbsp. of the olive oil, salt, rosemary leaves, and pepper.

Bake in the preheated oven for 30 minutes, until golden brown. Cool slightly, then drizzle the remaining olive oil over the top.

Chafing the dough: Hold the dough and curve your hands around it and use your palms to pull at the sides gently while you slowly rotate it, letting your fingers meet underneath. You should be left with a neat, smooth ball.

Watermelon Antipasti

Justin Hamilton, chef at LTK Bar and Kitchen
Boston, MA
www.ltkbarandkitchen.com

Serves 4–6

1 cup seedless watermelon, cut into 1" cubes
8 oz. fresh buffalo mozzarella cheese, sliced into ½" rings
¼ lb. Parma prosciutto, thinly sliced

Arrange watermelon, cheese, and prosciutto on a plate, "shingling" the ingredients (overlapping one of each). Repeat until all ingredients are used.

Sweet Balsamic Syrup:

2 cups balsamic vinegar
2 tbsp. granulated sugar

Add balsamic vinegar and sugar to a saucepan. Bring the mixture to a boil over high heat. Reduce heat and simmer, stirring occasionally, until the liquid is reduced by half. Turn off heat when liquid coats the back of a spoon.

Drizzle the prosciutto plate with the sweet balsamic syrup.

Salt-Crusted Chicken
Justin Hamilton

Serves 4

1 3–5-lb. chicken
1 cup extra virgin olive oil
   Freshly ground black pepper to taste
8 cups coarsely ground sea salt
1 sprig of rosemary
1 bunch of basil

Preheat oven to 375 degrees.

Rub chicken with oil, season with freshly ground pepper and a small amount of the salt, making sure to season the inside of the chicken. Place rosemary and basil inside of chicken. Set the chicken in a roasting pan, then cover the entire chicken with the rest of the salt until it is thickly coated. Roast for 35–40 minutes until the chicken is cooked. Remove from the oven and break off the salt rub before serving.

RECIPES

Tiramisu
Justin Hamilton

Serves 6

2 egg whites
4 egg yolks
1¼ cup confectioner's sugar
1¾ cups mascarpone cheese
3 cups extra strong coffee (brew twice as much coffee to water)
2 oz. Frangelico
2 oz. Myers's dark rum
7 oz. ladyfingers (approximately 1 package)
2 cups cocoa powder
1 Hershey's milk chocolate bar

Stiffly whisk the egg whites in a bowl until they form peaks. In a different bowl, beat the egg yolks and confectioner's sugar together until pale and fluffy. Gently fold the mascarpone cheese into the yolk mixture, then slowly fold in the egg whites, making sure that all the ingredients are well blended but still fluffy.

Mix the coffee, Frangelico, and rum in a flat-bottom pan. Dip each ladyfinger completely into the coffee mixture and then arrange on the bottom of a deep, rectangular serving dish.

Spread a layer of mascarpone cream over the ladyfingers and then sprinkle cocoa powder over the top. Repeat this layering process until the dish is full, and finish with a dusting of cocoa powder.

Using a fine grater, grate chocolate bar over the top of cake.

Cover with plastic or foil, making sure not to get the plastic stuck to the top of cake. Chill for three or more hours before serving.